Catching Two Frogs
With One Hand

Kon Blacke

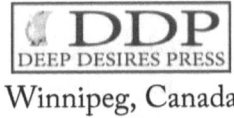

DDP
DEEP DESIRES PRESS

Winnipeg, Canada

Developmental editor Francisco Feliciano
Proofreader: Margaret Larson

Published June 2023 by Deep Desires Press, an imprint of Story Perfect Inc.

Deep Desires Press
PO Box 51053 Tyndall Park
Winnipeg, Manitoba R2X 3B0
Canada

Visit http://www.deepdesirespress.com for more scorching hot erotica and erotic romance.

Subscribe to our email newsletter to get notified of all our hot new releases, sales, and giveaways! Visit deepdesirespress.com/newsletter to sign up today!

Catching Two Frogs
With One Hand

First Course

Tetsu still couldn't believe he'd agreed to this.

More so, when one of the diners stated, "Hmm, this looks like a tasty little piece of sashimi, doesn't it?"

He sucked in a breath as the chopsticks pinched him in a place he didn't expect. "Um...I don't mean to be disrespectful, sir, but that's my foreskin you've got there."

The man grinned knowingly, eyes glistening. "Exactly."

"Oh."

And that's when Tetsu's mind had to go back. Back to when this crazy ride began...

The city streets were bustling, the air cool with a breeze lifting papers, leaves, and other detritus in little eddies around Tetsu and his boyfriend Rion as they walked toward their destination—a late-night sushi and saké restaurant they'd heard of named *Dankon no yorokobi*.

Which, from his understanding of Japanese, roughly translated to "pleasure of the phallus" and that was more than enough to make Tetsu want to go there with Rion.

As they walked closely together, brushing shoulders, touching fingers, he noticed most of the people around were couples enjoying a night out as much as they were. Most were holding hands too. As such, Tetsu felt the compulsion to stop teasing with his contact and grab Rion's hand properly; they were on a date, after all. If he couldn't hold his boyfriend's hand, tell the world he had one too, then what was the point?

In reply, obviously feeling the same, Rion laced his fingers within Tetsu's as soon as they became connected.

A strange but welcome warmth overcame Tetsu as a result, tingling where they touched. And yes, he knew why he felt like that. It was because of Rion. And if the man he now held hands with suddenly got down onto one knee to present a glittery ring dazzling brightly like an evening star under the lights off all the restaurants all around them, Tetsu would scream "fuck yes" and then kiss him with plenty of tongue, wandering hands, and a promise of more to come.

And that's not to say they hadn't done things with each other before now, either. Over the past few weeks, he'd gotten close to Rion. Really close. Not only had they kissed and exchanged blowjobs—now that's something special, isn't it?—they'd even had sex. Actual dick in hole, thrust, thrust, thrust, sweating, panting, jizz everywhere sex! Sex that was both awkward, painful, pleasurable, and surreal at the same time considering it was Tetsu's first time bottoming.

After all, Rion had no small shrimp between his legs; Tetsu was sore the next day. Worth it though. Being close like that was mind-blowing. An out of body experience too. He knew he'd get used to it, the physical side of their intimacy, because he'd never felt like this about any other guy before. A guy he most certainly wanted to show his affection for in public tonight.

He sighed happily, swinging his arm that held Rion's hand.

Rion, a red-headed, popular and pretty boy since forever, was his boyfriend. For real, his boyfriend! Tetsu still couldn't believe it. Being a nerdy boy, glasses-wearing to complete that look, painfully thin, pimples in random places all over his face, especially when he stressed—which was often—most other guys never even looked at him, let alone asked him out on a date.

Rion had been the only one.

His first in every way.

And as such, Tetsu would do just about anything for Rion, including holding his hand in public even if it meant getting hate from the homophobes.

Thankfully, there weren't any of those sorts around tonight.

Approaching *Dankon no yorokobi*, an out of the way establishment, down an alley and deeper into the gay district to the point of almost not being within it, Rion pulled Tetsu into an embrace under the building's simple entrance awning.

"What's this for?" Tetsu asked, giggling, feeling giddy and weak-kneed within his boyfriend's hold while returning the affection.

"Just because."

"I've got to love your spontaneity, Rion." Tetsu kept giggling.

Rion looked serious. "I love *you*, Tetsu."

And those words absolutely stunned Tetsu. "Wait... what?"

"You heard, baby." Rion smiled to his dusty emerald eyes.

Before Tetsu could reply, offer the return "I love you too" that was hanging from the tip of his tongue, because that's how he felt about Rion, truly, a short in stature man, dressed nicely but looking flustered, interrupted their moment.

With a grab of their shoulders, trembling, the man blurted, "Please hurry—I didn't realize you'd be so late. My word, why didn't you tell me you'd be late?"

Tetsu looked at Rion, then back at the man, more than puzzled. "Um...what are you talking about, sir?"

"You were supposed to be here a half an hour ago!" the man continued unabated, a vein bulging at his temple. "Don't you realize this puts me in a rather difficult predicament. Now please, do hurry. There's not much time."

Rion, clearing his throat, said, "I really think you've mistaken us for someone else, mister."

A blink from the man...like the click of a ticking clock attached to a bomb, really. Tetsu wondered when the explosion would result—*Boom!*

"I'm sorry, but as I've said, we've got absolutely no idea what you're talking about, sir," Tetsu had to say to try and diffuse the man's visibly growing tension. "We're not who you think we are."

That time, instead of rising tension—Tetsu believing a coronary was averted even though the man was beetroot red, right down his neck too—there was a change of expression; an understanding perhaps?

Breathing in, clearly calming himself, he said, "You're...you both...you're *not* the models the agency sent me for tonight's banquet?"

Hallelujah! The man did understand. Although, for the life of him, Tetsu couldn't imagine how they'd have been mistaken for models in the first place. Okay, maybe Rion. But certainly not him.

Not a chance.

Again, Tetsu looked at Rion before returning his attention to one, now very flustered and upset, restaurant owner.

Rion shrugged.

The man, introducing himself as Mister Nakamori, the owner of *Dankon no yorokobi*, then said the most surprising thing, "I don't suppose you'd be willing to work for a couple of hours, hmm? I'm rather desperate here."

Rion shrugged again. "Sure, we can wait a few tables for you, no biggie. I mean, we could do with some cash, being college students. Right, Tetsu?"

Tetsu wasn't so sure; he was on a date with Rion, after all. "I don't know about this, Rion."

"Oh, please, *please,* say yes," Mister Nakamori begged, his eyes also pleading, hands clasped in prayer almost. "I'll pay you as handsomely as you both are."

"Handsomely, huh?" Rion let go of Tetsu's hand, folding his arms after that, trying to be assertive with his body language. "What exactly do you mean by that, Mister Nakamori?"

A blink, a look around, a bead of sweat dripping from his brow, before replying, "I'll pay you five-hundred dollars each, not including the tips you'll get from the diners. That's how desperate I am, let me tell you."

Tetsu almost fainted, wishing he was still holding Rion's hand. "Did I just hear you say *five-hundred*...dollars each for a couple of hours work, sir?"

Mister Nakamori quickly, desperately nodded. "You did, yes. But you must come as quickly as you can; the banquet my most esteemed guests are attending starts soon and they don't like to be disappointed."

Rion beamed a smile. "Easy money, hey, Tetsu! Let's do it!"

But Tetsu wasn't so sure...again. "What sort of waiting work pays *that much* money?"

And that's when his imagination journeyed down a winding river to places that he would have never thought of before this moment. Places where scantily clad waiters served randy old business men, too drunk to stand, in smoke-filled rooms reeking of sweat and alcohol, doing their best to keep their butts from being pinched or spanked every time they bent over.

Tetsu's mind boggled, it really did.

Of course, what Mister Nakamori said in reply wasn't even in the same direction as to where Tetsu's thoughts had led him, the complete compass opposite to be honest.

He said, "My restaurant specializes in nantamoiri dining, and tonight we've got a special function on for some very important men. That's why I'm so desperate, as it's obvious to me now that the models I originally hired aren't going to show up. Not at all."

"Nantamoiri?" Rion asked.

But Tetsu knew what that meant...to his growing concern.

He swallowed, explaining, "Nyotaimori is when people eat sushi, sashimi, and other Japanese delicacies off the naked body of a presented woman, while 'nantaimori' is eating off a man...or in our case, eat such things off *us*. If we agree to it."

"That's correct," Mister Nakamori stated. "So please, I need to get you both prepared before the guests arrive soon. Please, I'll make sure you're tipped generously too. Very generously."

Tetsu's mind was spinning.

It was Rion who said, "Sure. I mean, it'll be a bit of fun, right? And what's more, five hundred bucks is five-hundred bucks. I'm not going to turn that down. Heck, I'd get my gear off for half that much, no worries. Anything more than that is a bonus. Right, Tetsu?"

But for Tetsu, it wasn't the idea of being naked in front of complete strangers...okay, maybe it was...but what happened during the dining experience that worried him. He'd heard stories about nantamoiri guests and the things they did to "appreciate" the models, both during *and* after the meal.

But in the end, Rion was right. If they were going to start their lives together, money was going to play the biggest part of that reality. They wanted their own apartment, if nothing else. And that took a lot of money to get set up. A lot.

"Fine." With a huff of resignation, doubts still circling within him though, Tetsu agreed with a nod. "I'll do it. But seeing as you're so desperate as you claim, sir, make it seven-fifty each and you've got your models for tonight."

Mister Nakamori's eyebrows shot up his forehead to disappear within his hairline. "My, my, you're breaking my balls here, boys!"

"Better yours than ours," Tetsu shot back, realizing his testicles would soon get very close to numerous pinching chopsticks, no doubt. He squirmed at that thought. "So…do we have a deal, or not?"

The man gulped. "All right, I agree. Seven hundred and fifty dollars each."

"We want it all in cash, plus any tips too," Rion chimed in, moving to hold Tetsu's hand once more.

Rion's gesture was appreciated, because if this was happening, unbelievable as it was, then Tetsu was glad he was doing such a weird thing with his boyfriend by his side, that's for sure.

And no, he would never forget this.

Still, memories were built from experiences, and for Tetsu this sure was turning out to be a memorable one. Hands down the most memorable of their relationship so far—aside from their bedroom activities, naturally.

Mister Nakamori bowed. "Agreed. Now please, let me show you to the shower room so that you can cleanse your bodies before you're plated up for my esteemed guests."

Tetsu once more looked at Rion. "Some date we're on, huh?"

"I promise I'll make it up to you later, but—"

"*But* the money was too good to pass up, am I right?" Tetsu interrupted.

Rion blushed but held his confidence, shoulders back, chest expanded. "That's right." He squeezed Tetsu's hand, which to him seemed like an apology.

One Tetsu accepted.

From there, Mister Nakamori took Tetsu and Rion into the restaurant via the back door, the one facing the alley way not the main street. It wasn't a glamorous entrance, the stench of rubbish bins, cigarette butts scattered everywhere, feral cat stink, and various cooking smells from the restaurant combined into an awful funk. One that turned Tetsu's stomach. Then again, he imaged having food eaten off his naked body was even less glamorous than that.

"I hope we get lots of tips," he whispered into Rion's ear.

"Same here."

Although Tetsu couldn't believe he'd agreed to this.

Being chewed out by his boss wasn't Hank's idea of a good time. He got the job done and caught the bad guys, helping put seven assholes belonging to an underworld gang behind bars, where they belonged. Sure, how he achieved that was rather unorthodox—involving a seriously disturbed ex-con to help get the information he needed without approval— but the result was all that mattered to him.

Seemed Superintendent Carter didn't get that.

To be frank, the man kept going on and on, really giving Hank the beans, which left him standing there, eyes ahead, hands clasped behind his back, and wondering when the man would come up for air.

"...You were reckless, Hank. You put lives in danger. *Civilian lives*. That's not good enough."

"But, sir!" he had to interject to make it look like he was listening...or cared about what the man thought.

It was all a moot point, anyway. Hank had been given a promotion to Inspector not long after his successful sting, so this was just the Superintendent letting off steam before he changed departments.

Hank couldn't wait.

"Jesus, don't 'but sir' me." Carter sighed, rubbing his temples. "We'll talk about this later, Hank—I need a few antacids dissolved in something harder than water right about now."

"Later" meant never, of course. Still, Carter had put him in a bad mood. Hank went home as grumpy as hell and feeling like shit as soon as he was dismissed.

What a fucking day.

The worst.

To add more to the steaming pile of crap he had to deal with lately all because he'd been doing his job, so involved he didn't even get time to scratch his own balls, Judy had broken up with him. She'd found another man. Hank, to be honest, was happy for her, even though the breakup stung, big time.

"I wish you well, Judy, I honestly do," he said pecking

her on her cheek, accepting her decision; one he couldn't blame her for.

"Ya not worried I ain't gonna be suckin' ya fat cock no more?" she questioned, frowning, hands on hips.

"I don't deserve you—and I wish you well with your new boyfriend. I really do."

She smiled. "I suppose ya can learn ta do it yo'self, huh?"

Hank chuckled. "I'll never have a woman as good as you, Judy. And just saying, I'll always love you."

She harrumphed, but not out of disdain, Hank knowing her little quirks well enough to recognize such a thing as affection. "I fuckin' hate ya, ya bastard, 'cause ya so noble and shit." She then kissed him tenderly on his lips, the taste of her cherry lipstick upon them intoxicating. "I'm leavin' now, otherwise I won't never go."

"I understand."

Their parting was bittersweet.

He watched her go, stared at his front door for ages once she'd closed it. When enough time passed, the hollow feeling really opening up, he decided he needed a drink to fill the gap.

A bloody strong one.

Several, more than likely.

And for whatever reason, not really understanding himself, Hank found himself at the last place on earth he ever believed he'd go to. The dazzling neon sign of the gay gentleman's club *Badda-Bings* greeted him, leaking its garish colors all over the rain-soaked building, the puddles on the ground, and the people waiting; it was like a night-time rainbow saturating everything with its joy against the gloom.

Hank proceeded to the front of the queue, not wanting to join the masses waiting to get inside.

"Holy crap, what are ya doin' here, Hank?" one of the security men Hank recognized and knew asked, the man glancing around nervously, shifting his weight.

"Don't stress, Rojer." Hank patted him on his shoulder. "This isn't a business call. I'm just here to grab a drink and then be on my merry way. Okay?"

"I see." A look of relief, above all else. "Um...did ya wanna see the boss, then?"

"Sure." Hank shrugged. "But I'll grab that drink first."

"Right ya are, then." Rojer unclipped the red velvet rope barrier so Hank could pass. "I'll let him know you're here."

"No worries—take your time."

Inside the club Hank knew well, a classy establishment exquisitely decorated with tasteful and functional furniture, he made his way to the bar through the crowd. And even though he never came here on social visits, the owner Michael, his boyfriend Tachibana, Michael's son Jake, and Jake's boyfriend, Larry, were all like family to him.

More than that, being honest.

If it wasn't for them, he wouldn't have been promoted. He'd also have never gotten chewed out by Superintendent Carter, either, but that was beside the point. Hank did what Hank did, which was doing whatever it took to catch the fucking bad guys. End of story.

He smiled at that thought.

At the bar, ordering a double scotch on the rocks, he sat, mulling over the past few days in his head, turning the glass, ice clinking, not even drinking except for occasional sips. In fact, while doing so, Hank realized that he simply liked being here because he wasn't bothered—most knew he was a cop.

The other reason being he wasn't sitting on his couch at home feeling sorry for himself. And that thought hit him the hardest. Because yeah, he was now alone, very much so.

And as if to rub salt into the wound of that realization, he had no one to celebrate his promotion with, either. His family, meaning Michael, Tachibana, Jake, and Larry, were all no doubt doing their own thing, rightly so. Besides, he hadn't told anyone about his new job yet either, so there was that as well. Not anyone's fault but his own.

As it *had* all been his fault about the way things turned out.

Hank sighed. He was about to get up, head over to Michael's office to remedy the situation, talk to him, to someone, when a young blond-haired man, sparking blue eyes and a smile that made him look interested and not just going through the motions, asked, "Are you married, handsome?"

The young man sat down, his hand sliding across the ridiculously shiny and ultra-smooth marble-made bar top toward Hank's which held his glass. The boy *was* making himself more comfortable, for sure.

That was kinda cute though.

Hank also found it amusing he was being hit on— didn't this guy know he was cop? *And* a straight one at that.

Then again, it wasn't like Hank was wearing a sign…or his badge.

"Nah, I'm single. Why?" he found himself saying, not believing how he sounded like he was leading this boy on.

What was going on?

"That's good, 'cause I'm single as well," was the answer, the smile of his widening to almost fill the room. It was that delightful. He then glanced down at what Hank was drinking. "Did you want another one of those? I'll buy it for you."

"I'm good, thanks." Hank covered the glass with his other hand, the gesture matching the intention of his words, but also admitting to himself he found this all too amusing. "What's your name, *boy*?" Because yeah, he was painfully young for Hank—no more than twenty, give or take a year or two.

"I'm Mason." The word "boy" didn't seem to faze him, not missing a beat of the conversation as a result. "And just so you know, I'm old enough for you to wear me like I'm your coat, but also young enough to be your good boy and for you to be my daddy…if that's what you want."

Again, and before Hank's brain caught up with what the fuck Mason was saying, he blurted, "What if I don't want a good boy?"

A raise of eyebrows, Mason's glorious smile fading to a dirty smirk. "Then I can be your bad boy."

Hank snorted. "I'm sure," he said, meaning to say he wasn't interested without actually saying the words.

But was he though—not interested?

As if by some turn of fate, Mason didn't seem to get

the intention, moving so his hand clasped Hank's where little tingles of "what the fuck was going on" coursed through him because of that touch, that leading gesture that was both unexpected but nice at the same time.

"I'm sure too," the boy replied, his voice turning sultry, amazingly so.

Hank sucked in a breath, surprising himself how affected he'd become within Mason's attention. Because yeah, the boy's contact, gentle and rather innocuous really on outward appearances, was far more erotic than Hank had ever experienced. It sent him into a spin. Truly.

What the hell?

Was it because such affection came from another man? Something far more salacious, more daring, more...*taboo* than what he'd experienced with women before now. Because here was a guy, so much younger than him, suddenly interested in him. Hank didn't know what to do.

He did know he wasn't repulsed. At that thought, he shook his head gently. Everything had become so surreal lately.

But as Mason's touch gained intent, the room around Hank then seemed to close in, the air turning thick too. He almost couldn't breathe. And what's more, all he saw now, all he could think about, was how there was this boy holding his hand tightly. Hank swallowed hard.

This wasn't right...was it?

Slowly, daring himself to, really, he looked into Mason's eyes, those brightly blue tainted waters, they were calling to him of a promise yet to come, to become drowned within them. And much to his continuing astonishment and disbelief, drown Hank did.

Through trembling lips, heart thumping hard, cock stirring, he uttered, "Then how about you show me just how dirty you can be?"

Mason quickly replied, "With pleasure, handsome."

After draining his glass, feeling the burn of the alcohol down to his stomach to warm him unlike anything else, that was when Hank found himself within a private booth, door locked, Mason on his knees, eyes glistening as he looked up while deepthroating Hank's rock-hard and throbbing cock.

And to make things even more surprising, as if they weren't already, Mason gave Hank a blowjob unlike any other. With Judy it was all patience and technique, teasing too. But with Mason, there was none of that. He was all about suction and taking it in as much as he could, saliva dripping, moaning, gagging, not caring how he looked, eyes watering, face flushed as he gave it his best.

And Hank sure appreciated that, no darn fucking doubt.

Did all gay men suck cock like this? Fucking hell if they did. Wowsers! What a rush! Like a storm wreaking havoc, it was. So different, almost like the night to the day.

Hank couldn't feel anything other than Mason's mouth upon him, that, and the ache, the rising joy coursing through him as he made the climb toward release. Sweet, sweet, release.

"I'm not...g-going to last long, you keep that up... boy!"

But that's when Hank became concerned. What was

the etiquette here? Was he to just let go, shoot his jizz down the boy's throat, then pat him on the head and shake his hand as a thank you very much? Give a bro hug perhaps?

Or was there more to it than that?

To answer him, Mason came off Hank with a loud popping sound, his lips, chin and face wet with his efforts, saliva dripping, delightfully so, What a turn on receiving such a messy, carnally fuelled blowjob.

Mason wiped himself with the back of his hand, his dirty smirk even more so. "How about you feed that thick piece of meat into my hungry ass then, handsome?"

God, that sounded so corny but so fucking hot too.

Before Hank could blink, Mason was standing before him as naked as the day he was born, holding a condom and maintaining his eager expression, more so than before. And aside from being nicely built, not too skinny or muscular, what Hank noticed most of all was that the boy was uncut, his foreskin half covering his already swollen knob, revealing more of it as he hardened. He was leaking too, a long clear thread of it. That was most certainly a different sight.

But most of all, Hank could only wonder when the boy had disrobed and where he'd gotten the rubber from? Did Hank blank out for a moment, his cock having been sucked so awesomely the reason for that?

He just didn't know.

Although he knew he felt giddy, realizing he'd reached out to pull Mason closer to him, bring him into an embrace, loving the feeling of their naked chests in contact. Their heat combined. Really loving it, in fact. It was intoxicating to the point of blindness, truly.

Mason moaned, holding onto Hank around his shoulders, mouth open, breathing hard, eager, rubbing himself up against him too. Holy smokes, it sure was a different feeling being so close to another man, smelling his musk, feeling his taut muscles, his relative roughness compared to a woman's softness. Also, there was that all too noticeable erection of Mason's pressing against Hank. Pressing harder and harder with each passing moment. So bloody different.

"Fuck!" Hank had to say, quivering all over now.

"I take it you want me?" Mason whispered into Hank's ear, nibbling on the shell of it.

Hank went weak at the knees from that. "I do."

"Then sit down on the couch, handsome," Mason suggested. "Let me ride you as hard as you need me to so you cum like a fire hose just for me, your bad, bad boy."

Hank went all giddy.

But as he looked deeply into Mason's eyes once more, something struck Hank. Something nagging at him but now coming to the forefront of his thoughts, his worries.

He had to say, "I've...not been with another man in this way...before. Just...just so you know."

Mason moved so he could look directly at Hank too, his expression turning to concern, shockingly so, like he'd been down this road before many, many times. "What...are you saying?"

And again, that's when Hank felt something other than his own lust overwhelm him. He felt guilt. Guilt because he didn't believe he could give Mason what he deserved, what he needed.

Because the boy clearly needed love.

That much was clear despite the bravado, the desperate blowjob to do his best, his eagerness to please. But Hank didn't want a relationship. Not so soon after Judy had walked out on him, anyway.

Hank felt himself deflate, not just physically. "I'm sorry…Mason. I-I can't do this. Sorry…" And he let go of the boy to pull up his underwear and jeans, zipping them up. "Really sorry."

"What did…what did I do w-wrong?" Mason's bottom lips quivered, eyes wide with both shock and sudden heartbreak.

"It's not you…it's me." And as Hank said that, he couldn't believe how fucking lame it was; he never thought in a million years he'd be using that shit reason on anyone, but there it was.

He was an asshole.

The ripples of hurt in the boy's blue, blue eyes after that slayed Hank to every fibre of every muscle within him, beyond that really. Nothing more needed to be said though. Nothing. He'd hurt Mason, plain and simple.

Hank felt like a cunt.

Second Course

Tetsu and Rion were escorted to a small floor-to-ceiling clean white-tiled room with an open shower. There were cupboards and potted bamboo plants scattered here and there; rather traditional Japanese-looking in a way. There was also a large mirror, white-framed.

"After you have cleaned yourselves thoroughly in the shower with soap, you'll need to use this to sanitize your bodies." Mister Nakamori picked up a bottle from off one of the cupboard's benchtops. "After that, I'll take you into the dining room so that you can be plated up for the diners."

"What is it?" Rion asked, taking the bottle and examining it by opening the lid to smell the contents. "Smells like some sorta disinfectant to me."

"It *is* disinfectant," the man replied with a slight bow. "Food grade and skin safe too, I assure you."

"Smells mildly citrusy to me," Tetsu commented after also examining the bottle once Rion gave it to him, scrunching up his nose.

"Yes, yes. Citrus is one of the several base scents people associate with cleanliness. Disinfecting yourselves with this after you've washed will reassure the diners that you've both been prepared properly, and that they can enjoy their experience here."

"I see." Rion looked at Tetsu, then back to Mister

Nakamori. "And I know we're going to be naked, but when you say 'disinfected after washing ourselves', do you mean that we've gotta be disinfected *everywhere*?"

"I do, yes," Mister Nakamori said, again a slight bow. "Oh, and if you're uncircumcised, gentlemen, please also make sure that you're cleaned and disinfected underneath your foreskins. As I said, every product I have here is skin safe and can be used even in the most sensitive areas."

Tetsu blurted, "Um…please tell me the diners aren't going to eat sushi off my dick." Ripples of apprehension coursed through him. "And besides, I can assure you it's clean underneath mine, Mister Nakamori—I'm *very* fussy about that sort of thing."

"Me too," Rion chimed in. "'Cause, oh my God, dick cheese is gross, *so* gross." A rancid look and a screwed-up nose followed those words to emphasize them.

Tetsu, nodding, moving to hold Rion's hand, loved that he could. "Unless you mean we have to have our foreskins pulled back for the diners, and that's why you said that. You know, have our knobs showing as a part of the whole presentation of things?"

What had he got himself in for?

Rion now looked slightly worried despite his earlier eagerness. "If that's the case, I ain't doing this. No way. If anyone's offended by any part of me, including not wanting to see my foreskin, then they can take a long walk off a short pier as far as I'm concerned."

Mister Nakamori raised his hands, offering the "calm down" gesture with a wide smile and more bows, lower and more respectful. "No one will be offended by anything; you are both handsome and attractive men. You will please them, very much so. I only said to make sure everywhere is washed and disinfected, just in case."

Tetsu was satisfied with that even though he had reservations and didn't quite understand what Mister Nakamori meant by "just in case".

"All right then," Tetsu finally said. "Let's do this before I change my mind."

"And get paid so we can get outta here ASAP!" Rion interjected, his enthusiasm returning. "Right, Tetsu?"

Tetsu heaved a breath. "Right."

Mister Nakamori bowed once more, backing out the door as he did so that time. "I'll return in ten minutes, gentlemen. Please make sure you're both prepared by then." He sounded enthusiastic as well, his smile adding to it. "I'll go check the kitchen to make sure the food's ready. And again, thank you for doing this, gentlemen. Thank you. Most appreciated. It truly is."

As soon as the bathroom door was closed, Tetsu grabbed Rion's other hand, bringing him closer so they were chest to chest, nose to nose, sharing breaths and warmth already.

"Are you sure about this?" Tetsu had to ask his boyfriend. "Look me straight in the eyes and tell me what you're really feeling, please. I need to hear it."

Rion did so, his eyes a wonder of dreamy emeralds. "I can't even *think straight* when I look at you in *any* way, Tetsu." His cheeks blushed bright red, redder than his hair. Very adorable. "But to answer your question, I *think* I'm sure. Yeah, pretty sure. Why?"

Tetsu could feel Rion's affection for him through their closeness, unbelievably and welcomingly so. "Perhaps it's nothing, but I didn't like how Mister Nakamori said 'just in case'." Unable to help himself, he brushed his lips against Rion's, a simple touch that always affected him so much, made him feel even closer to his boyfriend. "Because I think there's definitely something going on here that he's not telling us."

Rion moved so their contact deepened, kissing Tetsu, a kiss he reciprocated without hesitation, feeling warmer inside because of it, so loved as well.

Their kiss was eternal, even if only brief.

When parted, a little breathless, Rion whispered, "If you don't want to do this, we can bail. I know we need the money, but you're more important to me than anything else."

"I appreciate you saying that, thank you."

"Then what do you want to do?"

Tetsu, after deeper thought during more moments of gentle kissing, touching, squeezing hands, being close, replied, "This will be the first and last time, all right?"

"Of course, no worries."

"Good. And I'm glad you're on my side, Rion."

"There's no other side I wanna be on."

More sweet candy kisses between them; lips on lips with no tongues. Tetsu didn't need a rush of dizzying hormones, saliva shared with Rion to get him really turned on, and the resulting boner before having food placed upon his naked body if they open-mouth kissed now. Not at all.

And from the way Rion didn't pursue deeper contact, he imagined his boyfriend felt the same way.

They quickly moved away from each other, Rion looking flushed as Tetsu turned on the shower. A shiver of what could have been with Rion—so close to letting himself be taken away by the moment—ran through Tetsu.

Thankfully from there, getting prepared happened without further incident, even if Tetsu harbored a semi all thanks to being so close to Rion while naked.

Or he thought so...until Mister Nakamori returned, looked them both over, eyes wide. "My, my, I can see you're both rather big boys too, aren't you? You will most certainly please the guests tonight, no doubt about that."

Tetsu immediately moved to cover himself, more out of instinct under scrutiny than embarrassment. He was certainly not ashamed of his body. Not at all. He just didn't like the way the man stared at him, like he *was* the food, not the plate it would be served upon.

Although Rion, being Rion, stood with his hands on his hips, moving his body so that his proud dick swung from side to side. "The diners won't mistake *this* for no slice of raw sashimi, will they, huh?"

A polite bow accompanied by a contented smile was offered by Mister Nakamori. "No, no, they most certainly won't be mistaking it for that. All they will see are two stunningly handsome men presented for their dining pleasure, and I'm so pleased you have agreed to do this. So pleased." Mister Nakamori then gestured for them to follow, his expression holding upon his lips.

To Tetsu, that could only mean that the man was not

only happy with what he saw, he was excited that his paying diners would be as well.

Rion grabbed Tetsu's hand, something appreciated once more, that's for sure. "No matter what, I'm here for you, Tetsu," he said gently.

"Me too." And that was no lie.

None at all.

They were led to a lavish dining hall, entering it through a perfectly black lacquered wooden door carved with dragons and adorned with golden fittings. From there, if Tetsu wasn't going to be a part of the long room-spanning dining table, exquisitely decorated, he would have believed he didn't belong.

The opulence within the room was so decadent it hurt his eyes, truly. The dark walls were decorated with Japanese artworks, most traditional, of mountains, rice fields, and cranes flying above. There were also statues of those terracotta warriors, real or reproduced, Tetsu couldn't tell. Of course, potted bamboo was also present; good luck charms for the prosperity of the business along with painted paper lanterns and talismans Tetsu believed.

It was overwhelming how much was in the room.

Two men waiting by the other side of the door, dressed impeccably, bowties and everything, bowed low as soon as Tetsu and Rion entered properly.

"Irasshaimase," the two men chimed in unison, meaning that Tetsu and Rion were to enter and were welcome. "We are honored by your presence here, tonight," they added.

Tetsu, even though naked and greeted, honored, too, it

seemed, felt uncomfortable and exposed all of a sudden. The reality of what he'd gotten himself into becoming all too apparent. How many people were going to see his privates tonight?

Typically, Rion simply smiled.

Mister Nakamori, as if a raised voice would disturb the opulent atmosphere of the imposing dining room, stated quietly, "These two gentlemen will help you both get into place upon the table; please allow them to touch you."

Tetsu reluctantly gave his permission with a quick nod.

Before he knew it, he was gently assisted with efficiency to where he was to be placed before being plated up for the diners, only a few words spoken to ensure he was comfortable. Tetsu admitted he was…well, as much as he could be, considering the circumstances. At least he no longer held a semi, anyway. That disappeared long ago. Thank God.

Although, being presented on exquisite wood and expensive silken cushions, like a centrepiece of great value and importance, was kind of nice too. Also, having Rion positioned so he could see him, his head next to Tetsu's, was the biggest comfort of them all.

Perhaps this wasn't going to be so bad.

As soon as the assistants left, many people entered the dining room, carrying plates of food on silver platters. Lots and lots of food.

Mister Nakamori said, "Please, from now on, gentleman, can you both stay as still as you can. Everything must be perfect for our guests tonight. Perfect."

"Okay," Rion replied, pressing one corner of his lips together.

Tetsu knew what that meant—his boyfriend now wanted to get on with it. Tetsu couldn't blame him.

He felt the same.

At least the room was warm enough to be naked. And aside from the occasional whiff of the citrus disinfectant he'd rubbed all over himself as the sushi, sashimi, and other delicacies, including ura-maki, were placed carefully on his skin by many hands—the placing of them in certain spots, like over his nipples, tickled him sometimes—he wasn't hating what was going on. Thank goodness the food wasn't too cold.

When "plated", as it was known, the kitchen staff scurried away, bowing. Mister Nakamori clapped his hands, and his two assistants left the dining room, returning moments later with about a dozen men, all middle-aged and older, wearing business suits and serious expressions. There was nothing of note about them, faceless really. Like looking at the crowd on a peak hour train.

"Please, my honored guests, enjoy your meal," Mister Nakamori announced as the men sat cross-legged on the floor, traditional Japanese dining style, around the table Tetsu and Rion were laid upon for them.

All bowed respectfully.

And even before the first chopsticks were picked up, there were comments of appreciation and admiration from the men, their delight at what was presented for them clear.

Tetsu couldn't help but smile when one of them, "glasses and a nice face" he'd call him, whispered, "You are the most beautiful boy I've ever seen. And my goodness, you're worthy of more than ten times what you've been paid to do this for us."

From there, Tetsu felt something being placed into his hand. If he wasn't mistaken, it was a wad of money. A big wad.

Okay, he *could* get used to this.

Not only that, Rion was given money as well after being complimented more personally, all of them loving the redness of his hair; that on his head, his treasure trail, and pubes.

When a lot of the sushi and sashimi was eaten, one of the men, bald and big lipped, all squinty-eyed too, asked, "Are you two boyfriends perhaps?"

Tetsu knew he could speak, as he'd been asked a question. "We are, sir."

Nods and grunts of approval from the diners.

Another man said, "Can you kiss each other for us?"

Rion interjected, "Yeah, sure we can, sir."

And from there, Tetsu turned his head slightly to meet Rion's wanting lips. That time, there was a glancing of tongues, a tingle of wicked delight too, as if what they were doing was both salacious and daring. A thrill with an audience, no doubt.

But they didn't deepen their kiss too much.

Again, they both understood now wasn't the time or place to get an erection or get too heated. Not at all.

When parted, another man said, "That was most pleasing to see."

Tetsu, wet-lipped and feeling giddy, was surprised

when more money was placed into his hands, more than he could hold now.

"Yes, you are correct, Yukkon. It *is* most pleasing to see that Mister Nakamori has finally gotten it right when it comes to the boys he presents us for his nantamoiri dinners," the glasses and pleasant-faced man chimed in to grunting agreement from the others. "We were about to give up on them—a disaster they were before now."

"I'm glad we didn't give up on these dinners now," another said, his voice deeper and dripping with lust, Tetsu believed. "This has been a most pleasing evening. Most pleasing."

But from the direction of that voice, Tetsu then sucked in a breath as chopsticks pinched him in a place he didn't expect. "Um...I don't mean to be disrespectful, sir, but that's my foreskin you've got there."

The deep-voiced man came into view, grinning knowingly, eyes glistening. "Exactly."

"Oh."

Another, the one referred to as Yukkon, Tetsu believed, added, "Would you mind if we got you both excited so that you can season the last few pieces of sushi with your ejaculate for us, boys?"

"You'll be paid handsomely for it, naturally," deep-voiced man added.

Rion replied, "Whatever you want, sir. I'm game."

"All right," Tetsu said.

But Tetsu wasn't so sure and wanted to remind his boyfriend that this wasn't a part of the deal. Although before he could speak any of his thoughts, in protest or otherwise, that's when he felt a hand upon him. A surprisingly gentle hand grabbing his dick.

"Please, kiss each other again while we milk you for your special seasoning sauce, boys. Thank you," Yukkon said.

After that, Tetsu's mind went blank.

What with the heat of the room, seemingly hotter now, the men all around him, praising him, admiring him, and Rion's hot lips pressed against his, Tetsu felt the gentle stirrings within him that meant only one thing...he was climbing close to climax.

And as if to hurry things along, Rion soon deepened his kiss when Tetsu opened his mouth wider, saliva already dripping with his enthusiasm and arousal. He was beginning to breath harder, writhe upon the table, feel the familiar rush. The man masturbating him gained more purpose. He was good. So good.

Tetsu moaned.

There were more grunts of approval.

More groaning, more kissing, more light-headedness. God, this was both weird and erotic all at the same time. But before he could think about anything else, that's when Tetsu let go. Let go of everything. With a leg-slapping shudder, one, two, three, four times, he squirted his sticky jizz all over the many rolls of sushi a few of the men held in place for him to do so upon.

Rion must have ejaculated as well, his grunts unmistakable.

They parted their kiss, a string of saliva still connecting them for a moment, Tetsu's lips tingling as much as the rest of him, his dick most of all. What a rush. What a surreal experience as well. Wow. There were no other words to describe what had happened.

None at all.

Moments after that, and before their cum cooled and congealed, the "seasoned" sushi were all eaten to grins of approval and nods of appreciation. Lips were licked as well. More bowing. More money was given as well, most of it placed onto Tetsu's nakedness where the food used to be.

More admiration most of all.

"Having our sushi freshly seasoned by good-looking and fit boys is so much tastier than using wasabi or soy sauce, am I right, gentlemen?" the glasses and kind faced man said, still licking his lips, eyes bright.

Agreement from all of them.

The bald-headed man, standing, then announced, "We hope to see you both next Saturday night, boys. You will be here for us again, won't you?"

Tetsu found himself replying, "Yes, sir. We will be."

"Excellent—and what are your names, please?"

"Tetsu," Tetsu replied, "And my boyfriend's name is Rion."

"We are pleased with you both, Tetsu-kun and Rion-kun. Very pleased. Thank you for providing us with a most enjoyable and memorable evening tonight."

All of the men bowed low.

The bald-headed man, clearly their boss, gestured for the others to stand; they did so without hesitation, bowing to him, Tetsu, and Rion in turn again.

"Come gentleman, the dinner is now completed. We

will leave these two handsome boys to clean themselves up and be attended to by the staff here. It's time to enjoy a cigar and a glass or two of Mister Nakamori's best saké."

They all exited the dining room, following their boss like fledgling ducks did with their mother, the man named Yukkon winking at them before he departed the room. Tetsu still couldn't believe what happened. So strange, there was almost no way to fully describe it.

When alone for the few moments before Mister Nakamori's staff entered, Tetsu said, "Rion?"

"Yeah, Tetsu."

"What just happened?"

Tetsu heard the sound of money being counted, lots and lots of money. "I don't rightly know, but I've got over two-thousand dollars for whatever it was that just happened."

"I think I could get used to this."

Rion snorted a laugh. "You don't regret what we did?"

Tetsu had to admit he didn't. "I mean, what other job pays two grand each for only a couple of hours work?" Because he was sure he'd have about the same as Rion had.

"Too right," Rion agreed.

"And next Saturday night we can earn the same—perhaps more."

"Now you're talking…and all we have to do is let dirty old men jerk us off so they can season their sushi." Rion kissed Tetsu on the cheek. "I mean, by the end of a few weeks we'll have enough for a deposit on an apartment, this is that crazy. Seriously."

"Now *that* I can get behind—we can be together all the time in our own place for real."

"Like how I'm going to get behind you as soon as we get outta here?"

"Oh, are you now?"

Rion shrugged, his cheeks flushing. "I am."

Tetsu sat up, looking at Rion properly. "I *suppose* your decision for us to do this turned out to be a good one, after all. So yes, I'll bottom for you. But can you promise me one thing?"

"What's that?"

"We not eat sushi...*ever*."

"I hear that!"

They both laughed.

The door opened. The two assistants and Mister Nakamori entered the dining room. Tetsu and Rion were quickly helped off the table, while Mister Nakamori wore a smile unlike any other. It positively beamed, as if it were a lighthouse's light amongst the gloom of craggy rocks and dangerous waters. Tetsu knew why. They'd basically saved his ass tonight.

The man owed them...big time.

Hank didn't see Mason again after the boy hastily dressed and left the private booth, not even after searching the club high and low. He'd disappeared completely. Gone. Fuck, Hank didn't even get a chance to explain himself...or apologize. He felt like shit, guts churning terribly, more so than earlier.

He decided to go home.

What else was there to do?

Besides, his first assignment as an Inspector would be given to him tomorrow; at least that was something to look forward to. When home, relieved, he grabbed a bottle of beer, flopped himself onto the couch, unzipped, and while guzzling the amber liquid, refreshing and needed, with his other hand he jacked himself off to relieve the stress and built-up pressure of the day.

He finished before the bottle was emptied.

It was then, while still within his post-orgasmic haze, clinging to him as much as his guilt, that he realized it was Mason who'd worked him up so much. *Mason*. A guy. A *younger* guy no less, one who was not only sweet and adorable trying to please, but had surprisingly made Hank as horny as fuck because of all that too. In fact, without doubt, Hank craved more.

A lot more.

He had to find Mason. At least apologize to him, ask him if they could start over—if the boy would accept that, of course. Because it was then Hank also realized something else. He needed someone. And if that certain someone so happened to be Mason, then so be it.

"Fuck...I'm into guys too!" Hank said to himself, once he could see the bottom of the bottle, the thick lines of his jizz up his stomach to his hairy chest were visible through the glass. The stain on himself that completed his newfound realization...and guilt.

He got up, heading for the shower.

When undressed properly, the bleach-y smell of his

ejaculate fuelling his guilt further, he stepped into the steaming stream. "And for sure Mason deserves someone who'll treat him right—as I will treat him right if he gives me a chance. That much I know for fucking sure now."

Hank showered.

That night he dreamt of Mason, those bluest of blue eyes looking up at him, his hard cock deep in the boy's, dripping with saliva, mouth from his eager effort, begging for more, making swallowing, sucking, and those little gagging noises too.

"Yes, that's it." Hank said quivering with delight, scrunching up Mason's hair in his fists as he held onto him, admired him. "Suck me off like that, my dirty boy."

Groans from Mason in reply.

When the boy eventually came off Hank with a slurp, lips wet, face wetter, his lust-filled voice breathed, "Now breed me like I'm truly yours, daddy. Please, please fuck me hard. As hard as you can, 'cause I need you so badly I can't wait no more. Please."

Hank shivered again with delight, his hard cock glistening, twitching too. "I'll do just that. But first, bring that fucking cute ass of yours over here—I wanna eat it out to get it all nice and ready for my cock, boy."

"Yes, daddy."

From there, Hank imagined he was feasting on what Mason offered him, waking with a start as he came to a massive conclusion. Sweating, breathing hard, he sat up, lifting the covers and looking within his boxer briefs.

"Fucking hell, I had a wet dream like I'm some horny teen! Jesus! I've got it bad for Mason."

Another shower was needed.

By morning, Hank was exhausted.

He'd dreamt of Mason and what he was going to do to him many more times throughout the disturbed night, sheets wet, himself even wetter. Although, every single time he did so, he knew one thing.

He liked being called daddy by an eager boy.

That was fucking hot, to be honest. Very hot. And to hear Mason say it with that innocent and adorable voice of his, his less than innocent eyes looking lovingly at him too, was giving him a semi already.

"Calm the fuck down, will ya!" Hank chastised himself, shaking his head as he made his way toward the kitchen.

After breakfast of toast, coffee, and a side of guilt, because he didn't know for the life of him where he could even begin his search for Mason to explain himself to the boy, he climbed into his car, heading for his new department.

It was in the same building as his old position—the main station—but on a different floor. One that was, thankfully, far enough away from Superintendent Carter to avoid the man if need be. Which would be all the time as far as Hank was concerned. If he didn't see him for the rest of his life, it'd be too soon.

His new boss, Chief Inspector Schellenberger, was a portly man with fingers resembling painfully swollen sausages as he held onto Hank's file after retrieving it from his desk's top drawer.

"Vot vee have here izz interesting, Inspector Riley."

Hank imagined the man was either unaware it was his first day or was testing him, because for the life of him he had no idea what the Chief Inspector was talking about.

"Err...excuse me, sir. With respect, what's interesting?"

A look from above the open folder. "Zhat zhere izz confirmed gangland activity going on in zertain bars and restaurants within zee gay district, so our informants tell us."

"I see." Hank didn't see, but he was sure he'd soon discover it.

And what he found out wasn't exactly what he'd have thought either, because Chief Inspector Schellenberger, without skipping a beat, explained, "And zeeing as you're one of zhem, I vant you to take on zhis case, Inspector Riley."

Hank sucked in a heavy breath of surprise, suspecting what the man was insinuating even though he replied, "I'm one of *who* exactly, sir?"

And he wasn't sure whether or not he should be offended by that. Sure, he was getting his first assignment, a job which actually sounded interesting and something he'd want to do, but even so. This wasn't exactly starting things on the right footing, was it?

A moment of the Chief Inspector studying him, before, "You're a gay man, correct? As zuch, I vant you to get inside zee gang's circle of trust to get information on any future activities from zhem. Vot else vould I have meant?"

Hank blinked; he couldn't think of any other response he'd suddenly become that shocked. "I'm a *what* now?"

A raise of an eyebrow. "Did you not patronize *Badda-Bings* last night to engage yourself vith another man, hmm?"

As soon as his boss spoke those words, Hank's stomach sank like a stone was plopped into it. He felt woozy. Of course, they'd have been watching him; they'd want to know everything, every detail, about the man they'd recruited. That's how things worked.

"I...did," Hank admitted, feeling a flush of heat.

Not from embarrassment but of being so easily spied upon without his knowledge, he realized.

How stupid was he?

Although the Chief Inspector continued unperturbed, "Zhat izz vhy I zhink you're perfect for zhis assignment, Inspector Riley. And no offence vas intended—diversity helps us, not hinders. I apologize if I came across vith any disrespect."

"You...you know about me being with...with Mason?"

The Chief Inspector nodded, his jowls wobbling as he did so, like a bowl of jelly would once disturbed, hypnotic really. "Vee do."

But Hank, to clear the air and his own head most of all, had to say, needed to say, "I'm not gay. But you're right about one thing, because after I'd spent time with Mason," he snorted a sad chuckle, missing the boy so much, "I realize that I'm...bisexual. I'm a bisexual man who has only recently begun to understand himself, even after thirty-two years of being on God's green earth. A bloody surprise to me, but one of relief now that I've finally found myself, that's for sure."

And to admit all that to anyone, including himself,

lifted a weight from off his shoulders. Weight he didn't even realize he was carrying. What a moment. Hank was almost brought to tears, truly, his emotions were charging through him that much. He certainly got that lump thing happening in his throat, that's for sure.

But the reaction wasn't one Hank expected.

There was a smile from the Chief Inspector, almost not seen because of his plump face, but there. "I'm a bisexual man as vell, my friend." Now the smile was seen, beaming from him, radiating like revealing sunlight to bathe the room in its beauty and chase away the darkness.

Hank looked up. "Oh, um…okay."

Chief Inspector Schellenberger handed Hank the file. "You vill start immediately on zhis case, as zee undervorld activity izz gaining momentum lately, much to my annoyance. From our intelligence, zhere izz a gathering every Saturday night at zee restaurant called *Dankon no yorokobi*. Make sure you're ready by zhen. Do vhat you must to infiltrate zheir ranks to gain information."

Hank took the file. "Including sucking any cocks needing sucking, right?" He then laughed.

More smiles. "Do vhatever it takes—and from your past record, I know vithout doubt you're zee man for zhis job."

"Yes, sir." Hank looked up. "And thank you, sir."

"You are most velcome, Inspector Riley."

Hank knew of only one way to even begin his new assignment, and that was to contact the ex-con and police protected informant, Joe. He hated how it had come to that already, but he wasn't left with much choice.

He sighed. Joe was going to be a prick about Hank having to ask him for help again so soon. And yes, Saturday may be a week away, but there was a lot to do and not much time to do it in. Gaining enough trust in such a short time wasn't going to be easy. Impossible really.

But Hank had to give it a shot.

Joe wasn't difficult to find.

He was in a protected apartment under house arrest in the Docklands area by the bay. A small place, guarded, but hidden well enough for those not knowing what to look for to keep things low key. Perfect, really.

After the usual formalities, revealing their hate for one another all too well, Hank got down to business.

It was what he was visiting for.

"With no bullshit smeared all over it, Joe," Hank began. "Just tell me how I can get myself seated at the next gang meeting's table. The ones being held at *Dankon no yorokobi*, the sushi restaurant and bar. I need to get close enough to get information out of them."

A raise of eyebrows, right up to the man's long blond hair. "Now that's going to cost you."

A heavy sigh and roll of eyes. "What do you want this time?"

Joe rubbed his chin in thought, all overdramatic and as annoying as hell. Hank wanted to punch his lights out already. Honest.

The ex-con began, "Even though Jake's lovely cum-stained underwear you got him to give me are my most prized possession, I so enjoy smelling them let me tell you... helps me get to sleep at night, no kidding, I want a lot more than that this time. A *lot* more."

"Forget it," Hank spat. "Fucking forget it! You're not getting any poor boy to have your sick fun with. Just tell me what I need to know, you bastard. Otherwise, it'll be a trip to the emergency department because you've accidently fallen all over my fists."

Joe waggled his index finger. "Tsk, tsk, be nice, Hank. From what I heard, you were popping some cute boy's cherry at *Badda-Bings* last night. You wouldn't want me to spread around that juicy piece of knowledge to ruin your macho good cop reputation, now would you?"

"Fuck! What is this?" Hank gasped, feeling anger clawing at him all of a sudden. "I kiss a guy one time in my life, and every fucker on the planet gets an internet alert from Alexa! Jesus Christ, give me a break."

Joe shrugged. "Therefore, the price of my help will be you on your knees. Nothing less. Capeesh?" And there was most certainly a finality to the demand—one Hank couldn't ignore.

Hank, although jokingly had said he'd suck cock to his new boss to get the job done if needed, didn't believe for one moment he'd actually have to do it. And certainly not a cock belonging to a creep like Joe, either.

"Get fucked, Joe. That ain't happening."

Joe leaned forward, the leering expression he held clear. "I know where that pretty little boy you kissed, named Mason, works, if such information is worth your stupid pride, of course."

"How do *you* know that?"

"Oh please, give me more credit than that, Hank. I'm someone who gets off thinking about killing and then fucking twinks. Don't you think, just like how a lion knows where the zebras go to drink, that I would know where my prey are too, huh?"

Hank felt sick to his stomach, the draining sensation as he realized the horror of Joe's words overtaking him. "Now that you put it like that, yeah, I suppose you would know about such things."

He wanted to hurl chunks, he really did.

Joe continued unfazed, "And Mason sure is one tasty bit of prey, I might add. I bet he'd be finger licking good after being choked to death, no darn doubt."

Hank bunched up his fists. "Did you want that trip to emergency or not?"

Joe sat back in his easy chair, moving to unzip his jeans. Within a blink of an eye, he fished out his veiny cock, ugly in comparison to Mason's…to anyone's really.

Hank felt disgust wash all through him.

"You know what to do." The bastard smiled knowingly. "And my lips are sealed until you make me cum. That's the deal, take it or leave it, Hank."

"Can't I just give you a handjob and be done with it?"

"Nope."

"Then…I don't…I've not given a guy a blowjob before…" Hank admitted, feeling himself flush with both hatred for Joe and embarrassment because he was unprepared for this eventuality. Okay, he knew the mechanics of what to do, who didn't, but the actual technique, that mystified him in a way.

How did Mason do it to him again?

Hank felt the room spin as he got down onto his knees, staring at the throbbing hard-on Joe held for him to service, one that leaked a dew drop of pre-cum in expectation as if to really rub it in.

What a day this had turned out to be already. Fuck!

Joe laughed. "Then start how you think, and I'll give you pointers as you go. All right?"

"Fine—but this isn't going to be a lovey-dovey blowjob if that's what you're expecting."

"I expect to blow my load down your throat and that's all, so get on with it."

"Just shut the fuck up, huh!"

Hank moved so he could get close enough to at least lick Joe's cock with enough enthusiasm to make do, shuddering with disgust as he did so. Still. He had to get on with it if he wanted the information from the bastard. If anything, finding out where Mason worked suddenly seemed more important than anything else. And that was a surprise.

While Hank licked cock, hours seemed to pass.

It was excruciating.

He noticed Joe wasn't even getting into it. That was his problem. Hank was doing enough. More than enough, really. And then with even more rasps of his tongue over Joe's knob, tasting salty, he licked some more, almost feeling sick to his guts.

But that didn't seem good enough for the bastard, as his next words attested to. "It's not a fucking clit, Hank."

The man laughed; the barking sound as annoying as he was. "You've got to stop licking it at some stage and get it into your mouth! Don't be shy. It's only a cock. So, get on with it and suck it, man. Now!"

"I fucking hate you," Hank mumbled around Joe's hardness.

"Whatever. Just don't forget to use plenty of spit and suction. Dry mouthing isn't hot, no matter what anyone thinks."

Hank hocked and spat, landing a huge globule onto Joe's swollen knob, now dribbling wet with his spit. "Like that, fucker?"

"It'll do."

"You really piss me off, you bastard—but sure, I'll do what you want. I'll suck your cock like you want me to if it'll get me the information I need."

"Such dedication to duty. It brings a tear to my eye, it really does."

"I can change your circumcision status all too easily with one bite, you know," Hank growled, liking the idea that he sort of had the power here.

"Now, now. Keep playing nice. Uncle Joe has lots of information for you once he ejaculates. So how about you get on with it? There's a good boy."

Okay, maybe he didn't have any power.

None at all, really.

"I fucking hate your guts."

Joe snorted more laughter. "You've already established that. Now less talking and more sucking."

"Fine."

Hank, with anger, increasing hatred for what he had to do, and sheer unadulterated loathing for Joe, sucked and sucked, adding slurping noises and moans to try and get the bastard off as quick as possible. Hank also gripped his hand tightly around the man's veiny length, as hard as he could, tugging viciously at the same time he used his mouth. That'll teach the fucker if he expected a blowjob full of affection and sweet sensations.

Joe moaned, closing his eyes, lying back more.

Hank, surprised, realized the bastard was getting into what he did. Thank fuck. Because if it lasted much longer, Hank was sure his jaw would drop off any moment, it ached that much.

And despite having to go down on Joe, Hank knew without doubt this was not how it would be when it came for him to do such a thing for Mason. If he was given the chance to do so, of course. Because instead of disgust, contempt, and anger sprinkled with repugnance, there would be admiration.

Hank admired Mason.

And that would make all the difference, big time. Hank sure hoped Mason accepted his apology. Hoped beyond anything else, really.

"I'm...gonna cum!" Joe exclaimed suddenly, thrusting his hips to disturb Hank from his reverie.

Hank gagged on him because of the change in momentum, spitting, coughing. He really did hate the bastard. Thank fucking God this'll soon be over and done with.

He could tell Joe was close.

As such, Hank kept his lips around Joe's knob as best he could, bracing himself for impact, as it were. He became amused by that while he wondered what another guy's jizz would taste like. Sure, he knew his own. What man didn't? But another man's?

Hank wasn't kept guessing for long.

With shudders and shouting from Joe, calling loudly, "Take it all into your fucking dirty mouth, you slut," which was creepily different, Joe released and released…

…and released.

Hank, holding onto the man's pulsing cock as it delivered its ejaculate, almost choked on it again but for a different reason, spluttered, trying to swallow down the bleachy brine-tasting gooey mess that stung his tongue and numbed his mouth.

Hank's eyes watered and he felt himself heave many times.

This was disgusting!

Or more to the point, Joe's was disgusting.

When done, *finally*, Hank came off Joe's softening cock with a wet, sloppy popping sound, relieved it was done.

Never to be done so again, either.

His voice hoarse, still tasting bitter salt right to the back of this throat, Hank spat, "Now tell me fucking everything you know, including who I need to contact to get me a seat at the table for their next meeting."

Joe, smiling contentedly, beads of sweat on his brow, replied, "I warn you, Hank, this will be the last time I squeal like a pig for you. The *last* time. Next time you come calling for information out of me, I'm going to kill you then fuck your dead ass until I've embalmed you with my jizz. Got me?"

"Suits me fine." Hank got up off his knees, wiping his chin of Joe's filth, still cringing with disgust about what he'd done. "I don't ever want to see your ugly head again." He glanced down. "Either of them."

"I'm glad we agree." Joe zipped up after stuffing his cock back into his pants; Hank relieved he no longer had to look at it. "First, you'll need to get a hold of a man who goes by the name of Yukkon. Convince him you're one of them and he'll give you what you want. Give you anything, really."

"Where do I find this Yukkon fellow?"

"He operates an abattoir on wharf Road—I'll give you the contact number."

Hank was taken aback. "I didn't know there were any of those sorts of places operational around the Docklands anymore."

"There aren't." Joe sat back, knitting his fingers, remaining content with his expression. "It's a front for a sex slave market, one of the biggest in Melbourne. They mostly sell teenage boys groomed for the purpose, but sometimes they sell girls. Depends on the demand, really. But most buyers prefer boys; they're easy to fuck and there's no chance of them getting pregnant. Less hassle, to be sure."

Hank felt the room spin around him again, needing to steady himself. And just when he believed he couldn't feel any worse, he'd heard that. What a fucked-up world this was. No fucking lie.

"I bet you've bought a couple of boys from there in the past to kill and then fuck, haven't you?" And that time Hank really did spit his disgust at the ex-con he had to do the unthinkable with just to get this far.

Joe didn't seem to take the bait. He laughed. "The boys sold there can cost millions, depending on their age and how pretty they are. I wouldn't pay that kind of money for a boy who's not going to live long once I start having my wicked way with him, now would I?"

If at all possible, Hank felt even worse.

He really did want to puke all over Joe's carpet, great big chunky vomit marinated with Joe's jizz he'd just swallowed that didn't sit well within him all of a sudden.

Instead, Hank decided the better course of action was to get on with things instead of dwelling on the despicable nature of the men he was dealing with. Terrible men. Men who he couldn't wait to put behind bars.

"What do I need to do next, then?"

"If you're accepted into the gang, you won't need to do nothing more."

"Easy as that, huh?"

"No."

Hank eyed Joe. "What should I expect, then?"

Joe shrugged. "Knowing Yukkon, if you think sucking my cock weirded you out, then you'll be in for a surprise, that's for certain."

Hank didn't want to ask, but instead directed the conversation to the matter at hand. "Does Yukkon report to Mister Yaketsuku?"

"He doesn't," Joe replied quickly. "He reports to another man who in turn works for Mister Yaketsuku."

"What's this other man's name?"

"I don't know."

"You fucking do." Hank snorted his disbelief. "Now spit it out like you spat out all that cum of yours down my throat."

"Honestly, I don't know." And Hank knew he didn't. Joe wasn't known for holding back anything. He loved to sing like a canary; that's why he was used as an informant. "All I know is that it's Yukkon who's the one who organizes the dinners at that restaurant you mentioned. It's an establishment owned by one of the gang's 'stock replenishers', I might add; a greedy and insipid little weasel of a man named Mister Nakamori."

"Stock replenisher?"

"Yes, Mister Nakamori helps them procure the boys they'll sell in their market by grooming them. He does this by paying handsomely for what at first seems quite innocent on the face of it, but quickly turns into something far more sinister."

"Seems I've got my work cut out for me."

"Oh, but wait, there's more. Because I've heard on good authority that there are two new boys already caught within Mister Nakamori's clutches. They were lured in with an offer of a job no one applied for—Tetsu and Rion are their names. Stunningly handsome boys too, I've also heard. I feel sorry for them, I really do."

For Joe to feel sorry for anyone, that was something else. Truly. "Fuck," was all Hank offered as he realized his assignment had already expanded to include a rescue mission now.

Just his luck.

"Yes, fuck indeed." Joe's expression turned to sadness. "Any boy would rather have me end them quickly than be forced to suffer a life of sexual slavery, mark my words. The one I got caught for killing, believe it or not, Hank, that was his wish. Honest as the day is long. Honest."

"That doesn't justify murder, and you know it, Joe." Then Hank decided to change the subject to one far lighter. "How about you tell me where Mason works so we can finally end this little chat of ours."

"Ah, I wondered when we'd get to the real crux of our business."

"Just fucking tell me."

Joe laughed. "That desperate to get your cock into Mason, hey?" But before Hank could explode, fists flying like he wanted them to, the creep added, "He works at the flower shop, the one near Flinders Street Station."

Hank sucked in a breath, feeling giddy all of a sudden. Of course, Mason would work in a place like that. A place of beauty. A place where care and gentleness and love would be needed…no, required. So much like him, even if Hank had only known him for less than an hour.

An hour that changed everything, though.

Everything.

"Thanks, Joe," he said dreamily, thinking of Mason.

Joe sat up. "You love him, this Mason boy…don't you? I can see it in your eyes, the way you changed once we started talking about him. You've got it bad, my friend. That you have."

"Shut the fuck up."

Joe smiled, standing. "Goodbye, Hank. Never come back again."

"That's a deal."

Third Course

Tetsu kissed Rion, a wonderfully common thing lately. In fact, since last Saturday night he'd been on cloud nine. Not only did he feel so much closer to Rion, more in love with him, they had sex more often too. Hot, steamy, gasping for air, bodies intertwined, wonderful sex where nothing else mattered but each other.

He was not only getting used to bottoming for his boyfriend, he loved it too. The connection of the act that went beyond the physical. Deeper than anything, really.

Tetsu, relaying his thoughts, amused he did so, said, "I never thought I'd say this but I miss it when your dick's not inside me, Rion."

Rion chuckled, returning the kiss. "You love being a stuffed boy now, huh?"

"Yes, I do."

They both laughed.

"Say, what are you going to wear for tonight?" Tetsu asked, picking up a shirt then putting it down on the pile on the bed in front of him again, undecided about it.

They were in their bedroom at Tetsu's parent's house. A cramped room where the walls were paper thin and any intimate time had to be done as quietly as possible so as not to disturb the rest of the household. A house packed to the rafters of his siblings—he was the eldest of five. Tetsu couldn't wait for the day when they could move into their own place; if only for more bathroom time.

Rion shrugged. "Does it matter?"

"Well...considering we're soon going to be naked and covered in food so that wealthy business men can eat it all off us, it doesn't. Not really." He picked up one of the other shirts he'd discarded. "I'll wear this one, then."

"Good choice."

Tetsu leaned over to kiss Rion again. "I love you, Rion, you know that."

"Ah shit," Rion screwed up his face. "Why'd you spoil the moment by getting all sappy on me?"

Tetsu grabbed him around his slim waist, pushing him onto the bed, coming on top of him. "Don't be cheeky. Tell me you love me back."

"Or you'll do what, pray tell?"

Tetsu moved so he could pin Rion's arms down to tickle him, knowing all his vulnerable spots. "Or you'll suffer the consequences."

Rion was soon in fits of laughter, eyes watery too. "St... op! I...I give up. St...op!"

"Tell me you love me, and I will."

"All right, all right! I love you."

Tetsu kept tickling his boyfriend. "Say it like you mean it."

Rion was almost breathless he was laughing so much, in hysterics really. "I...love you! Okay? I love you, Tetsu! I do!"

Tetsu stopped. "That's much better." And with that he moved so his lips could brush against Rion's, asking for more kisses, deeper and more meaningful ones after that declaration.

When Rion had calmed enough, wiping his eyes, they were soon locked in an embrace, mouths opened for each other, writhing, becoming more and more heated as their passion and lust built between them in equal measure.

With the piles of clothing kicked off the bed, Tetsu and Rion shed their own. Now naked, intertwined, rubbing themselves against each other, Tetsu soon found he was as hard as ever, yearning, desiring, loving that Rion would soon be a part of him again already.

An unexpected and delightful turn of events for sure.

"Fuck me," Tetsu demanded, nibbling on the shell of Rion's ear, enjoying the smell of him, his natural odors combined with the perfume he wore, one that was spicy and woody at the same time, spurring him on even more.

"Ask me nicely, and I'll give you what you want," was his cheeky payback reply for the tickling earlier.

Tetsu loved how he'd said that. So sexy. He therefore moved so he could look Rion within his stunning green eyes, also loving how he could so easily, within a beat of his heart really, become lost within them too, wonderfully so.

"*Please* fuck me, Rion," Tetsu whispered, trembling with want.

Rion offered a wickedly seductive smile, one that whipped Tetsu into a frenzy even more while he ran his warm hands tenderly down Tetsu's back to cup his buttocks, massage them, nails raking, shivers of delight accompanying his touch.

"I've gotta say, you're becoming one very thirsty bottom boy, aren't you?"

Tetsu could not only feel his dick leaking, throbbing too, but his saliva thicken within his mouth as well. He was so horny. So needy. He really did want Rion. Wanted him like his blood craved the oxygen from his lungs.

"I'm only thirsty for you."

"That's good to know." Rion kissed Tetsu's lips, once, twice, three times. "But this time we're going to do things a bit differently."

Tetsu was both surprised and curious. Normally, along with all the kissing of course, they exchanged blowjobs before Rion would lay him down and fuck him missionary style; a position Tetsu loved because he could look at Rion, watch his expressions, enjoy his climb to the heights of his climax as much as he did.

"What do you mean?" Tetsu asked.

"I mean, I want you to sit on my dick, Tetsu. And while I'm fucking you, I not only want you to jerk yourself off, I want you to tell me how you're feeling. Make sure you talk dirty too while you get yourself really worked up. It'll be so hot, truly!"

"Oh, that *is* different."

"You'll love it." Rion brightened even more, beaming a lust-filled smile, cheeks reddening as much as his hair. "Now get to it, Tetsu. Moan for me, let me hear your thoughts and see you cum—drench me in it. Turn me on even more so I can shoot my load deep inside you so that I can claim you as mine again."

Tetsu found he was being turned on more and more by what Rion was saying. "You're right, I *am* yours."

"Then do it, baby."

"Yes, Rion," he replied while leaning over to grab the lube always on the bedside table.

From there, Tetsu applied it to Rion's hardness, getting him really slippery—he wanted to suck on his boyfriend, but that wasn't asked of him. Instead, he got on with what he was told to do, eagerly and with his own feelings of passion growing with each passing moment.

Tetsu quickly positioned himself so he could sit on Rion, opening his legs to not only touch himself as asked, but to let Rion clearly see what he was doing.

"That's it, like that," Rion said, shuddering already. "Now tell me how you're feeling before it goes inside you."

Tetsu took a moment to gather his thoughts. "I'm excited."

"I can see that, silly." A chuckle. And yes, Tetsu's erection wasn't hard to miss, the best gauge to his state of mind right now, for sure. "I want you to tell me how you're feeling, really describe it. All right?"

"Okay." And that's when Tetsu felt himself flush with warmth, making his cheeks numb, causing him to hesitate.

Rion sat up on his elbows. "Are you embarrassed I'm asking this of you?"

"No..." Tetsu gathered himself. "It's just...I've never done this before, that's all. I don't want to disappoint you."

"You will never disappoint me; don't ever think that, baby."

Tetsu felt more warmth, right to his balls that were

resting on Rion's hard stomach, feeling him quiver inside through them, their connection established already before penetration had even begun. "I...I'm not sure how to say it...I feel so much already."

Rion ran his hands over Tetsu's legs, tenderly and with pure love reflected in his eyes. "Let me tell you how I feel; we can then go from there, all right?"

Tetsu nodded, appreciating Rion's solution to his sudden dilemma—how to get in touch with his feelings while his body rushed with lust and everything else for what was to follow.

Rion explained, "At this very moment, I feel the weight of you on me as something that comforts me, and I love how your body heat and touch will be something I'll miss when I don't have you so close after this as well." He paused, moving his hips so that his erection rubbed against Tetsu's buttocks with more purpose, sending more delight all through Tetsu, unbelievably so. This was sexy. Very much so.

"Tell me more," Tetsu whispered, his voice hoarse with his passion.

"You can feel how I'm becoming more aroused by your butt cheeks surrounding my hard-on, can't you? 'Cause the anticipation I feel makes me blind to everything else— which is a good thing. I know my heart beats for you, Tetsu; even more so during these moments of our intimacy."

"Oh, God, that's...that's beautiful."

Rion winked. "Your turn now before you put my dick inside yourself for me, huh."

And even though the heat of being under such close

scrutiny still washed through him, Tetsu, touching his own hardness, moving his hand to stimulate himself even more, quivering, uttered, "I feel the need to have you is something that also gives me comfort. But at the same time, it goes beyond that. Because before I knew you, I felt lost and incomplete. And I know it sounds sappy to say this, but you've changed that for me. I never knew I needed someone like you to do that, either."

"Didn't think you'd be so in love, did you?"

"No."

"Then let me fuck you so we can consummate our feelings, baby."

"So much yes to that, Rion."

A moment passed, one of shaking hands and fluttering butterflies within his stomach, while Tetsu reached behind himself, grabbing Rion's slicked, warm, hard as a rock, dick.

"This is so hot," Rion writhed underneath Tetsu.

A sucking in of air through his teeth as he positioned himself to take Rion inside himself. Another moment. Then, sitting down, sinking his body onto Rion's erection, Tetsu felt that now familiar sensation, that pain, as his boyfriend's hardness pressed against his hole. He shuddered. Another moment of sharp and deep pain before he gently pushed out as he'd taught himself to do, something that caused Rion to become fully seated within him.

Tetsu moaned, breathing hard already as he took a moment to come to terms with the rush he felt, the blinding moment of such bliss and agony and wonder.

"Tell me what you're feeling now," Rion asked, moving his hips with more purpose.

"I...I feel overwhelmed. As you go fully inside me, there's a weird moment of pressure and pain, deep inside me, before I tell myself to relax and breathe."

"Yes, your tightness around me is amazing, that's for sure."

Tetsu began to masturbate himself with greater intent, loving how his foreskin helped lubricate his action, making him more sensitive, gaspingly so.

With lips quivering as much as the rest of him, feeling overwhelmed but beautifully so, he continued to describe things as he'd been told, "I can feel your big dick rubbing against my prostate, Rion. Oh...it's making me tingle all over and causing my legs to go numb, no lie." Tetsu had to take a moment to breathe. He gathered himself. "Oh God, Rion...you're...so huge, you're really filling me up while I'm in this position. It's so different...but so, so good! Ah! Ah! Mhm, I love it."

He then moved himself up and down so he was really riding Rion properly, just like how they did in those porn vids he used to enjoy before getting the real thing. He felt slutty but also, strangely, amazed at how good it was to experience sex in such a position.

To make it even more erotic, hot as hell really, Tetsu's mouth salivated like nothing else. He even had watery eyes, aching nipples, and of course, not only was his dick leaking, making a little wet patch on Rion's stomach, glistening, he could feel his balls tighten.

"Good boy," Rion encouraged. "Ride me hard, baby.

Keep going. But don't forget to talk to me—I want to know everything. Even your most intimate thoughts."

Tetsu, his mind a muddle now as his body raged with not only the serotonin rush as he watched Rion underneath him, loving how his boyfriend was enjoying what was happening, but everything else as well, managed to say, "I... don't want this to end."

"Why not?"

Tetsu noticed a sheen of sweat forming on Rion's brow as he thrust upward with increasing vigor. "I...you being inside me like this...it makes me feel as though I'm a part of you. It makes me feel like I'm your whore and...and I love that feeling."

"You *are* my whore, baby."

"I love that I am."

"Now tell me more, please. This is really turning me on right now, let me tell you."

Tetsu stroked himself with more vigor, feeling his swollen knob tingle with the rest of him, amazingly so. "I can feel how you open me up, not just physically, but emotionally as well. And it's changed me for the better. It makes me happy."

"Fuck, yeah."

Tetsu then couldn't go on any longer. He had to let himself go. "I'm going to cum, Rion!"

"Describe it! Quick!"

"It's like a torrent inside me, swirling all though my deepest parts, rushing forward. It has to escape. Ah! I...I can't hold it back any longer. Oh, God! Rion...I...I—" At that moment, Tetsu ejaculated.

With a massive shudder, almost collapsing but stopping himself so Rion could see, he shot forth thick ribbons of his sticky white goodness all over his boyfriend's stomach, chest, chin, and face.

It went everywhere, even over the sheets.

Panting, flushed, euphoric, Tetsu sat back, trying to gather himself. He felt Rion inside him even more as he went even deeper because he'd done so. It was a buzz that enhanced his post orgasmic rush. He shuddered even more.

So good.

Rion began trembling with more purpose now too. "God, when you cum, you tighten up so much around me it's making me...fuck! I'm cumming too!"

And then Tetsu felt Rion release.

Soon, they were both done, hot, sweaty, and even more in love. Tetsu collapsed onto his boyfriend, holding him tightly, letting his jizz become the glue of their love between them, not caring it did, either. His mess was a thing of beauty because it was Rion who'd caused it.

And that was all that mattered.

After an eternity of just holding each other, the smell of their sex still intoxicating, pungent, Rion whispered, "You've really let yourself go completely for me, haven't you? And for that, I really do truly, honestly love you, Tetsu." Rion held Tetsu tighter, Tetsu feeling more than completed in his arms as a result. "With all my heart, I love you, baby."

"I love you with all of mine too, Rion."

After another long blissful moment, skin on skin, eyes never leaving each other's, punctuated with tender kisses, tongues and breathless moments, tasting of the salt and goodness of himself, Tetsu said, "But don't you think that we'd better get ready for work, hey?"

"Yeah, you're right—I don't think I can handle Mister Nakamori having a coronary again if we're late."

"Although, when we're in the shower I'd love to...you know, give you a blowjob...in thanks for being so amazing just then." As he said that, he could feel Rion's jizz leaking out of him. It was that sensation that turned him on even more. Made him want more already.

"Ooh, you *are* getting really dirty, aren't you?"

"You encourage me to be so."

Rion kissed Tetsu on the cheek. "I'm glad I do." He then spanked Tetsu on his buttocks, a loud *thwack!* the result.

Tetsu giggled, liking the sting he got, a sensation that made his dick perk up from its semi state. "I want to please you again, Rion."

"You are nothing but a pleasure to me."

"As you are to me."

The text message Hank sent at the beginning of the week to Yukkon remained unanswered. Not that he expected an answer straight away. It was always a waiting game, police work. Always.

And just like how his department had done before they recruited him, Yukkon's men would be watching him now that they knew about him.

No doubt they were watching him now.

It wasn't until he was out shopping on a sunny but cool Friday morning, mostly for beer and microwave meals, carrying it all in one of those fucking reusable cotton bags he had to buy because the free plastic ones were no longer provided, that he decided to walk to the corner of the street where the flower shop was located.

The same flower shop Mason worked in; if only to confirm he did. God, he missed Mason so much. Couldn't stop dreaming about the boy, either. As such, Hank had self-serviced himself that much over the past few days he swore he'd worn his fucking knob down to a stump.

Fuck, he had it bad.

But at the moment there'd be no respite from the agony of not being able to see Mason to talk to him, to apologize, even though it was confirmed Joe's words were true. Mason did work there. The boy was as beautiful as he remembered when he came out of the shop to replenish the outside display with care. He really was dreamy, his golden hair glowing in the sunlight, gentle face, tall and perfect really—better looking than Hank remembered, which was saying something.

Although at that thought, sadness soon found him.

For the here and now, he knew he couldn't contact Mason, much to his annoyed regret. The reason? He didn't want to involve him, wanting to keep him safe, because Yukkon's men *were* watching him. Hank knew this without a shadow of doubt because of the suspicious looking black Mercedes cruising past him many times already, slowing down before passing to go around the block again.

Such amateurs though, it made Hank laugh.

Really laugh.

Still, after he'd made contact with Yukkon, he'd offer his apology to Mason then. And yeah, when he thought about that, his heart thumped hard against the back of his ribs and he began to sweat, right to his palms.

He'd never apologized to anyone in his life before. And here he was, hardly able to wait for the moment when he could. That's how much Mason affected him

Affected him so much.

He was about to turn and leave, walk back toward his car, when his phone finally buzzed. A message from Yukkon...or one of his goons, anyway.

Don't move from where you are.

Hank texted back a simple thumbs up emoji.

A moment after hitting send, the sleek Mercedes that'd been tailing him all morning pulled up to the sidewalk, the passenger door opened.

"Get in," was all that was offered by the driver, leaning back to get a good look at Hank, and sounding serious.

This was it.

Hank did as he was told without delay, keen to get on with things. About fucking time really.

The car zoomed off before he could close the door completely.

When seated properly...well, as comfortable as he could get seeing as he felt like he'd been invited into a pit of vipers, he turned to look to his right. Next to him sat a middle-aged man wearing an expensive looking business suit, silk tie, gold cufflinks, white carnation, handsome in a creepy sort of way but with a receding hair line and a thin moustache that looked drawn on. Hank assumed he was Yukkon.

The man, his voice cool and almost sinister, simply asked, "What do you want to talk to me about?"

Hank put on his game voice straight away, getting to the point, "I hear you sell merchandise I might be interested in buying."

"You heard that, did you?"

"Yeah." Hank tried to calm, feeling his heart race even more than the brief moment he caught a glimpse of Mason earlier. "But how about we cut the bullshit, and you just tell me if you're willing to sell to me or not."

Yukkon studied Hank for a moment. "It's not that simple."

"Then simplify it."

"As you wish." Yukkon smiled, nothing but a scar across his face though. Hank shivered at the sight of it. "But before we begin, I'm letting you know I've checked your credentials. I hope you don't mind." Hank indicated with a shake of his head he didn't. Yukkon held his expression at that. "On first glance, I'm pleased you've passed our criteria; the real estate business is booming lately, isn't it?"

Hank was sure glad he'd set up one of his alternate identities well before this meeting, the department helping with that—including creating a fake bank account with millions in it to complete the ruse. He wished the money were all his though. Pity it wasn't.

"It is," he offered not wanting to divulge any additional information, blabber mouths always got caught out, and he didn't want to have to remember so many lies.

He already had to make sure he remembered his alternate name, George...George Armstrong Riewoldt. What a name! It would be hilarious if this situation wasn't so serious. Truly.

"Very well, George-san." The man seemed to relax. "Tell me, are you interested in buying a boy or a girl?"

"A boy, naturally," Hank replied knowing Yukkon mostly sold or auctioned off boys thanks to Joe's information. His next words emulated the ex-con too, "I don't want any unwanted brats running around the place getting in the way, now do I?"

"That's true, no denying that." Again, more ominous smiling. "But any girl you buy has the potential to give you a son. And it's that son who can then be trained from early on without the use of drugs to please you; a two for one bonus, if you want to look at it that way." He winked. "I've got a beautiful little boy at home who wants for nothing else but to give himself to me whenever I desire it."

Hank felt woozy. "How..." he cleared his throat, "...old is he?" He then realized he may have asked the wrong question at the wrong time because it sounded too cop-like, really.

He didn't want to raise suspicions already.

Yukkon didn't seem worried, or was distracted by his thoughts. Either way, what he said next was unbelievable. "Connor-chan is turning eight next month." A shift in weight; a sigh. "But I will have to dispose of him before he reaches puberty; I don't like them when they get that old. Pity. He is a favorite of mine." Another moment of thought.

"Then again, perhaps I can sell him off as used goods to get *something* for him instead of having to kill him. Perhaps."

What the actual fuck! Hank couldn't believe his ears. What's more, the car's interior spun around him, terribly so, after those words were spoken. He went all funny, almost to the point of blacking out. Such evil words spoken, the realization of what they meant, he just couldn't even begin to fathom. That poor kid caught in Yukkon's vile clutches, a sex slave from birth, had no life at all. Absolutely horrific. Beyond words, really. Beyond anything imaginable, to be truthful.

Hank wanted to kill this Yukkon character with his bare hands already, and he'd only known him five minutes. That was an achievement, for sure.

After that, Hank felt sick to his stomach, bile to his throat sick. But he had to keep himself calm even though he now wanted to reach over, grab one of the cocktail glasses set into a cabinet with champagne in front of him, then use it to gouge Yukkon's eyes out before ripping his balls out by their roots to feed them to him, his last meal before killing the bastard.

Yukkon deserved no less.

And to be honest, Hank couldn't think of anything other than that which would satisfy him after what he'd been told. Nothing at all. Jail was too good for him; Yukkon and his men who helped him all needed to be six feet under. The sooner the better too.

Instead, Hank replied, "All what you say is interesting, but I don't have the patience to train a boy for my particular needs. I want one ready to go as soon as possible."

"I understand." Yukkon nodded. "If it pleases you, I can take you to the warehouse that holds within it our stockroom right now. That way you can pick out a boy you like, because for most of them I can offer a 'buy it now' price before auction."

"Sounds peachy to me."

Yukkon leaned forward; to his driver he stated, "You know where to go, Maurice."

"Yes, sir," the driver replied efficiently, flicking on the indicator then turning the car onto the road leading out of the city and toward Docklands. The closer they got to the warehouse the more Hank felt nerves shred at every fibre of his being. He kinda loved the feeling though. It meant he was on the right track.

This was it.

Time to start bringing these bastards to justice.

After a moment, Yukkon added, "Although if you don't like any of the boys I have for sale in our stockroom, I do have a couple of potentials coming up who won't be there but will be ready soon. One is a redhead, the other, dark haired—boyfriends they are. They're very cute and very fit, with lovely sized uncut cocks on them too. If you're interested let me know, because they won't last long at the price, even if they go to auction."

"How much are they?—I wasn't planning on buying two." Hank tried to sound noncommittal even though Yukkon was clearly describing Tetsu and Rion.

He had to calm himself again.

"I'm willing to offer you a substantial discount if you buy the both of them together. Let's say...two million as their buy it now price and be done with it, hmm?" He moved closer to Hank. "What do you say to that deal, George-san?"

"Let me see the boys you've got in your stockroom first," Hank replied, playing the game as best he could...he hoped. "I don't want to miss out on seeing any who may meet my expectations before I make my choice."

Besides, the more evidence against the bastard he got the better, so he had to go to that stockroom and see it for himself. He would be lax if he didn't.

Yukkon sat back, no longer interested now money wasn't being spoken of, clearly. "Tell me, what kind of boy meets your expectations, then?"

Hank had to be careful not to describe Mason, that wouldn't be good. "One who knows his place and does what he's told," was his enigmatic response.

"I see."

Fearing his answer was too obscure, he hastily added, "And one who can suck cock and take it up the ass at any fucking time like a porn star, of course."

The sinister smile returned. "Of course."

Within no time, they were parked in front of a nondescript warehouse, windows painted over, and one that looked like all the others along the deserted docks. Hank got out of the car, glad for it. He breathed in deeply the fresh air.

Yukkon had his door opened for him by the driver, Maurice.

Together, Hank walking beside Yukkon, they entered the old building. Four men, serious expressions, most with tats all over them, greeted them. One or two had a concealed weapon, Hank knew. Pistols, no doubt. Illegal, but what did that matter to these bastards? They were selling people to be used as sex slaves, so carrying a gun would be a minor charge against them compared to that.

Beyond the sight of the welcoming committee, the warehouse was relatively empty. Abandoned. At first, Hank was both surprised and a little scared. Had he been found out? Were these men now going to murder him? Now would be a good time to do so. No witnesses.

"Gentlemen, this is Mister Riewoldt," Yukkon introduced. "He's interested in buying and is here this morning to inspect the merchandise we have on offer at the moment. Please treat him as our guest."

One of the men stepped forward, the one wearing shades indoors of all things. Hank wanted to punch them off his face, but calmed himself, even if he tightened his fists.

He said, "Which room do we unlock, sir?"

"The boys' room, please," Yukkon replied.

A nod.

After that, Hank was escorted by Yukkon and his men to the back of the warehouse that used to service its life as an abattoir. There were still remnants of that past left here and there, including meat hooks and rails above and a few remaining pens obviously used to hold the animals while they were being slaughtered.

Hank got a creeping dread feeling, hating the place even more already.

Through a heavy cool room door, once unlocked, Hank

was invited inside. Yukkon never left his side. Neither did the other men. There was no escape now, not even if he wanted it.

He was committed.

Once clear of the plastic curtain all meat work factories had somewhere, Hank's breath was taken from him by the sight of what he witnessed before him. In the massive room beyond, one that had served its previous life as a meat freezer no doubt, there were more than twenty cages lined up around the walls made of Perspex or some sort of tough glass for easier viewing.

He really was in a showroom's stockroom, wasn't he?

And aside from the air holes across the top of these purpose-built cages, straw lining the bottoms, each collared and chained naked boy within each was only provided with a steel bowl full of water. Hank then realized there was nowhere for them to go to the toilet. The boys couldn't really move much either, conditions for them were so cramped. How long had they been in these cages? The poor, poor boys. Holy fucking hell!

Hank felt so sorry for them all.

Because not only were they captured, kept in such inhumane and woeful conditions, their future uncertain, he knew by the way they didn't move much, respond to Hank's presence either, that each boy was drugged up to his eyeballs.

As Hank took in the unbelievable sight, finding it hard to process really, mindboggling to say the least, he realized the boys for sale ranged in ages from about eighteen to twenty-five, give or take a year or two. One or two of the boys looked suspiciously underage though, much to Hanks further disgust.

It was sickening to see, really.

Although he noticed all were slim to the point of almost being emaciated—clearly, they were only fed enough to keep them alive long enough before they were sold.

Hank's stomach sunk right to his feet.

Yukkon, as if he were talking about pets being sold in a pet shop, not boys, stated casually, "We've got a wide variety for you to choose from." He gestured to the nearest cage. "That one there is twenty-one years old—and as you can see, he's dark-haired and has a nicely cut dick. A guaranteed anal virgin too, I promise you that." Before Hank could comment, Yukkon moved his attention to a couple of cages beyond, stepping forward as he did so. "While the boy in this one is a cute blond, uncut, and only just recently turned eighteen. Most delicious, isn't he? Although, because of his age and looks, he'll fetch a lot more than his reserve. I'm hoping for three million, at least, for him."

"What's the buy it now price for him, then?"

"He's one of the ones not for presale; he's far too valuable for that, being so young, fresh, and tasty."

"I see—you do have a lot of stock here," Hank found himself saying, all his insides turning terribly. In all his years, he'd never seen the likes of this before, and on such a large scale too.

Why hadn't this been discovered before now? He then felt even worse, kinda blaming himself for what he saw. The pain he felt for the boys kidnapped and sold in such a way hurt him beyond any physical pain he'd ever felt. Truly, it went right to his bones.

"We try our best to provide as many different types of boys as possible. It creates more of a buying frenzy, you see."

"Good idea." Hank really wanted to throw up, and mustered up all his strength within himself to stop himself, honest to God.

"Thank you." Yukkon then pointed out a cage that was empty. "Here is where the two boys I mentioned earlier will be kept when they arrive. Of course, I've just got to finish grooming them, but they'll be ready soon."

"And how exactly do you groom the boys you'll then sell?" Because Hank, for the life of him, couldn't imagine anyone agreeing to this—not for all the money in the world.

Yukkon narrowed his eyes. "You ask many questions, George-san."

Hank knew he had to be careful here. "Who's parting with a cool two million bucks to get a regular fuck, then? You or me?"

Yukkon relaxed. "Very well. To answer you, they are groomed at our primary supply outlet, the *Dankon no yorokobi* restaurant. It's there where we find out if the boys Mister Nakamori chooses for us are receptive to our needs after being given gifts and money. If they are what we require, they'll then be drugged and brought here until auction if they're not sold beforehand."

So, in other words, the boys chosen were given bribes, abused under the guise of entertainment, kidnapped, drugged against their will, then sold to the highest bidder to become sex slaves. Hank hadn't lost the urge to choke the life out of Yukkon and his men, not by one iota.

He said, "I assume the boys will need to remain drugged, even after they've been sold."

"You are correct." Yukkon nodded. "A buyer will want their purchase to be receptive to their desires at all times even if the boy is out of it, so to speak. And besides, all sales include enough drugs for the lifetime of the boy they buy, that's also my personal guarantee."

Hank, much to his hatred and disgust, had to ask, "How long do they usually live once they're sold?"

"You *are* full of questions, aren't you?"

Hank shrugged. "You know my reasons."

Yukkon offered an accommodating bow. "I can assure you, the boy you purchase will live long enough for you to use him however you want before you get bored of him."

"I don't get bored easily."

"Then you administer a lesser amount of the drug each day." Now it was Yukkon's turn to shrug. "Perhaps you can get a couple of years value that way. I'm not sure. Most men who buy boys instead of training one from birth like I have, need to replace him after about six months or so, sometimes sooner."

Hank didn't need to be told that was the boy's life expectancy. "Fair enough," was all he could manage through lips suddenly dry, his whole world now a complete turnaround because of what he'd seen and heard, devastatingly so.

From there, he looked around the room once more, needing air all of a sudden again, feeling even worse but doing his best to keep himself composed. "Perhaps I'd like to see these two new arrivals instead. These boys here don't seem to suit my…particular needs."

Another scar-like smile. "I knew you'd be impressed by the fact one of the boys I'm grooming for sale is a redhead."

Hank had to play along still. "Yeah, I think a ginger will suit me just fine—you don't have any of those here, I see."

"Did you still want to purchase the redhead with his boyfriend before auction, or would you rather wait for it, see if you can get him cheaper?"

"I want to see them both first before I decide. I don't want no ugly boys sucking my cock, even if they're a bargain buy. Understand?"

"Oh, I completely understand." Yukkon, produced a business card from his suit's jacket pocket. "This is the address of the *Dankon no yorokobi* restaurant. Please join me there tomorrow night for dinner, George-san. The two boys you are clearly interested in will be there to entertain you as well as be open to your inspection. I'll make sure of it."

Hank took the card, flicking it over many times, nervously really, because he knew what he really wanted to do with his hands; strangulation of a certain bastard standing in front of him. In fact, he'd love to see the life ebbing out of Yukkon for what he'd done, that's for sure.

But Hank had to bide his time.

If he acted too soon, aroused suspicion already, he could place all of these boys, Tetsu and Rion included, in terrible danger. He had no doubt in his mind that Yukkon would order them all killed without so much as a thought, the perverted bastard—look at the way he spoke about his son, Connor, for fuck's sake!

More gut-wrenching hate found Hank.

Then Yukkon, once realizing he'd been discovered, would go to ground, perhaps never to be seen again, to start an operation somewhere else.

For now, and to prevent all that, Hank had to play along. And as much as he hated doing so with everything he had inside him, he had to do his job first and foremost. He also had to get justice for these boys with minimal risk to them. All of them. Thankfully, the first steps had been completed toward that goal.

He could now make a difference.

"Thanks for the invite, I'll be there," he said, pocketing the card.

And be there he would.

That way he'd know without any doubt who all the others involved were, from the beginning of the operation to the end of it, the full scope of this depravity Yukkon had created for his own twisted greed.

And as far as Hank was concerned, this whole sickening operation began at that restaurant, their "primary supply line" as it was referred to. Because knowing who this Mister Nakamori was, all the other players too, would be important to crack this case wide open.

In fact, if Hank had actual money to bet on it, he'd say this whole sex slavery operation was being controlled via Mister Yaketsuku, the bastard and gang boss he'd put in the slammer a while ago. And there was only one way to deal with a crook like him, and that was to cut the strings he controlled on the outside.

But one step at a time.

First, he had to rescue Tetsu and Rion…then the rest of these poor boys—and any girls too. After that, heads would roll. Big time.

Hank couldn't fucking wait.

Fourth Course

Arriving at Mister Nakamori's establishment within plenty of time of their arranged meeting, hand in hand, Tetsu still feeling the warmth of what they did together not that long ago, the soreness too, must have delighted the man.

The owner of the restaurant bowed low as soon as they entered. "I'm so glad you've both agreed to return for tonight's special event."

Rion retorted, "Aren't they all special?"

"Indeed, they are." Mister Nakamori gestured for them to follow him. "Now please, let me escort you both to the shower room so you can get yourselves prepared."

"You know this is going to cost you more than last time, Mister Nakamori," Rion said cheekily, squeezing Tetsu's hand.

Mister Nakamori smiled. "Money is of no importance, only the happiness of my guests is. And they are indeed happy with you both, so therefore I am as well."

Tetsu couldn't believe what he'd heard. "So...exactly how much are you going to pay us, then?"

Another polite bow. "How does a thousand dollars each sound for tonight's work?"

Again, Tetsu couldn't believe it, but before he could contemplate what he was being offered, comment on it either, Rion interjected, "You've got yourself a deal, Mister Nakamori."

The man looked at Tetsu. "Do you agree with this arrangement, young man?"

"From the large increase," Tetsu began, "I get the feeling you're asking more from us than simply taking off our clothes and having sushi eaten off our naked bodies. Am I right?"

Mister Nakamori blinked, distant for a moment, but ultimately offered a bow. "You are right—how very perceptive of you, Tetsu-kun."

Rion said, "What do you want us to do for that kind of money, then?" Again, another squeeze of Tetsu's hand, that one definitely more nervous, Tetsu sensing his anticipation through his contact too.

"If you were to perhaps engage in certain…sexual activities with each other for my guest's entertainment after their dining experience, it would be most appreciated. Most appreciated indeed."

Tetsu knew it…but also felt worry stab at him. "What *sort* of activities are you referring to?" Because now he wasn't so sure he wanted anyone seeing what he did with Rion other than kissing and holding his hand, of course.

Obviously sensing Tetsu's hesitation, the man said, "I can double the wage…no, I can triple it, if you say…got yourselves into the sixty-nine position upon the table to then perform blowjobs on each other. How does that sound?"

Rion looked at Tetsu, eyes wide. "What do you say to that, baby?"

"I'm...not sure."

Mister Nakamori, clearly concerned things weren't going his way, shifted his weight. "Oh, I'm sorry, I meant to say I'll pay you five thousand each for this. My mistake."

Tetsu sucked in a breath while Rion blurted, "Bloody hell, for ten grand I'd, like, fuck Tetsu on that dining table for everyone to see, no lie!"

"Rion!" Tetsu said, disbelieving.

Rion, offering a quizzical look, replied, "What does it matter if we show people how we love each other for money, Tetsu? It's not like they're gonna be joining in with us, is it?"

"Oh no," Mister Nakamori chimed in, "for that you'd be paid a lot more than ten thousand dollars."

Both Tetsu and Rion looked at the man; a moment of stunned silence was shared between them. Tetsu just didn't know what to say to that. To any of this, actually.

And because he remained quiet, neither did Rion, it seemed.

To finally break the stalemate, Mister Nakamori said gently, "You both must only do what you are comfortable with, there is no pressure here. But whatever you decide, you'll be paid accordingly. All right, boys?"

Tetsu, still processing things, feeling that nagging at the back of his mind, a warning perhaps, said, "I think we'll just play it all by ear for now."

A bow, deep and low. "As you please—now quickly, you need to prepare yourselves before our guests begin arriving, including one special guest who has asked to talk to you both before the dinner."

"Who's that, then?" Rion asked.

Mister Nakamori smiled, "A real estate mogul who goes by the name of George Riewoldt—very generous when it comes to opening his wallet for handsome men like you both are, I heard. Perhaps you know of him?"

Tetsu hadn't. "Fine, we'll meet with him. Right, Rion?"

Rion shrugged. "Yeah, whatever."

Another long bow from the restaurant owner. "I shall arrange it."

There was soft *rap, rap, rap* on the door of the shower room, right when Tetsu and Rion had begun disinfecting themselves after showering. Good timing—not! But no doubt the mystery man who wanted to see them had finally decided to make himself known.

"I reckon he waited until we got our gear off before knocking, hey?" Rion observed with a chuckle while Tetsu went to the door.

"I'd say you're right."

Tetsu opened the door, not caring that the man saw him in his birthday suit; it's not like he wasn't going to soon enough, anyway. Although when Tetsu spied who was on the other side, his heart sang and he couldn't believe his eyes.

"Hank!" Tetsu cried, quickly embracing the man without thought. "I can't believe it's you."

"Woah, easy there, buddy." Hank said, patting Tetsu on his back, twice quickly, before parting with a good arm's length between them. "I kinda think that was a bit too up-close and personal there considering your state of undress, huh!" Hank, looking puzzled, glanced over to Rion. "Say, why are you both starkers, anyway?"

Rion, shrugging before continuing to rub himself in the lemon-scented disinfectant, Tetsu liking the sight because his nipples glistened as a result, so sexy, replied, "We're getting ready for the dinner, why else would we be like this?"

More confusion from Hank. "I don't get it."

Tetsu asked, "I take it you've never been to a nantamoiri banquet before?"

"Not really. No."

Rion replied, "Well, Hank my man, you're soon going to find out, aren't you? But how we are now, naked and sporting semis, that's a big clue as to what to expect."

Tetsu agreed—even if his wasn't exactly a semi—but didn't add anything else to that track of the conversation. He was too distracted. Not only about why Hank was here, but because of the sight of Rion now applying the lotion to the rest of himself. Again, a lovely sight, mostly because the wetness of the disinfectant before it dried seemed to enhance is abdominal muscles and the other sexier parts of him rather nicely.

Tetsu thought so, anyway; and that's all that mattered, wasn't it?

"I suppose I *will* find out, yeah." Hank then entered the shower room proper but not before looking over his shoulder to check for something in the hallway beyond. He also closed the door. What exactly he was looking for out there, Tetsu didn't know.

This all seemed rather secretive.

When clearly happy they were alone or whatever, Hank, lowering his voice, continued, "I can't be gone too long without arousing suspicion, but listen up you two, I've got to tell you what's going on here."

"We're listening," Rion said, keenly.

"Good. 'Cause I'll say this only once," Hank replied.

Tetsu moved closer to Rion. "It's about Mister Nakamori, isn't it?"

With eyebrows raised, Hank nodded. "In a nutshell, Mister Nakamori acquires young men for an underworld gang's sex slave operation." Tetsu was about to open his mouth, shocked, Rion sucked in a breath too, when Hank raised his hand to stop him. "Please, guys, let me finish. Okay?"

Tetsu closed his mouth, only then realizing it was hanging open.

He knew his earlier doubts weren't for nothing, even if this was far worse than what he could've imagined. Then again, who in their wildest nightmares would have thought that this restaurant, seemingly innocuous on the face of it, was a front for an such an illegal operation?

No one ever.

Hank continued, "Unfortunately, because of your acceptance to be here, you've both been recognized as potentials for their purpose, which is why I'm here. I'm posing as a real estate millionaire wanting to buy you both."

Rion, through a trembling voice, grabbing Tetsu, holding his hand tightly, managed to say, "I...I can't believe this is happening." He looked at Hank, pleadingly. "Why is this happening to us, Hank?"

"I honestly don't know why, but it's happening," Hank said. "Anyway, I can't stay with you here for much longer. Just know that whatever happens, just trust me. Okay?"

Tetsu, also feeling the weight of all this upon him, crushingly so, replied, "Without any doubts at all, we trust you, Hank. Don't we, Rion?"

Rion only nodded in response.

"That's good." Hank composed himself for a moment, clearing his throat. "I've also got to tell you both to try and accept whatever they want you to do...within reason, of course. That way you won't put yourselves in any immediate danger. Got it?"

"Yeah, I got it," Rion piped up, voice croaky.

"Me too," Tetsu added, feeling worse than Rion sounded.

Hank smiled, even if it held uneasiness within it. "I want all of these bastards locked away for the rest of their natural lives, no fucking lie. And yeah, that'll happen if you guys keep your cool and keep playing along."

Tetsu wanted to walk right now, this was all getting too much for him. Rion as well, by the way he held his hand; tight, trembling, and sweaty as anything. Jittery too. As if he was ready to barge past Hank and bolt out of the restaurant's front door into the streets beyond, not caring about his state of undress, Tetsu going with him no matter what.

He had to say, "Um...Mister Nakamori just asked us if

Rion could fuck me for his guest's entertainment after the dinner."

"Shit." Hank seemed to sweat then, wiping his brow. "Look, I can't tell you to do anything you're uncomfortable with, but just think about what I've said. That's all I ask. I don't want either of you hurt."

"Okay, Hank," Rion said, still shaking but loosening his hold.

Tetsu was kind of relieved Hank was here looking out for them, no doubts about that. But at the same time, he had greater concerns. "But what if one of the guests asks if he can fuck me?" was Tetsu's question, one he had to ask because it had bubbled up from the darkest regions of his thoughts and needed answering. "Mister Nakamori has already offered a lot of money for me to consider such a thing."

"More like they all want to get their dicks into the both of us from the sound of it," Rion chimed in.

Again, Hank wiped his brow. "If that's the case, then I'll do whatever I need to do so that doesn't happen."

"How will you do that?" Tetsu questioned, once more that bubbling inside him, worse than thick black tar poisoning his mind.

"Do you really want me to answer?"

Rion said, "I reckon we do, yeah."

Hank heaved a deep breath. "Seeing as I'm here claiming I want to buy you both, I'll state that no one can touch you because you're mine."

"Oh…okay." Rion tightened his grip once more within Tetsu's hand.

Tetsu had so many more questions, but again, one particularly terrible one bobbled up above the chaos within him. "If it comes down to it, does that mean *you'll* have to fuck us to prove yourself, though?" He gulped after that.

In all honesty, Tetsu would rather have Hank do what he had to with them than anyone else...if there was no choice left, of course. No choice whatsoever.

Because yes, even though the money they'd been offered would be amazing to have, Tetsu realized it was all too good to be true now. Typical. If it glittered like gold, was it always gold? Not in this case. As such, he now wanted these men—Mister Nakamori definitely included—arrested and sent to jail for what they'd done. What they're doing now.

Another gulp but also a steel of his resolve.

Hank, opening his mouth to answer, was prevented from replying by Mister Nakamori suddenly opening the door. "Please, George-sama, enough time has been wasted." The man bowed deeply, never looking directly at Hank. "Your presence is required in the smoking room by Yukkon-sama, and I'll need to get Tetsu-kun and Rion-kun prepared for your dinner with them tonight."

And with that Hank left, leaving Rion and Tetsu alone with the most despicable man imaginable. Being near him again made Tetsu's skin crawl to make him feel uncomfortable in the worst way possible. How many young men had this evil man helped sell into a life of sexual slavery? He hated to even guess.

It was then Rion blurted, "Forget the sixty-nine thing,

Mister Nakamori. I'll fuck Tetsu for your guest's entertainment, but it'll cost you, cost you a lot!"

Tetsu could feel Rion's grip change as he spoke those words, like he was telling him something through their contact. If he didn't know any better, it was simply "trust me".

Tetsu did.

Always.

"My, my, they will be most pleased to hear this." Mister Nakamori beamed a greedy smile. "Because just like how kopi luwak is coffee that's made with beans passed out of a civet to give it a distinct flavor, sushi seasoned with ejaculate from a bottom boy's anus is just as so. It has a spicier tang." He paused in contemplation for a moment, eyeing Tetsu with a leering stare while doing so. "It's also a delicacy, and a favorite of mine, I admit."

Tetsu's skin no longer crawled; his whole body seemed to. What sort of sick men were these guys, Mister Nakamori included? "What about the money?" he asked to keep the conversation relevant.

"You will be paid most handsomely. Most handsomely indeed."

"How handsomely?" Rion questioned, still doing his hand thing.

The man's smile held. "Is seven thousand dollars each, handsome enough for you both?"

"Make it ten each, and it's a deal," Tetsu replied with determination, eyes narrowing but hoping above all hope Hank knew what he was doing.

Mister Nakamori bowed. "A deal is struck between us, I feel."

Hank entered the smoking room, a space which was an eclectic mix of Western and Japanese inspired themes, full of leather couches, potted bamboo, ornaments, and books within bookshelves lining all of the walls but one.

There were eight other men present.

"What did you think of the merchandise, George-san?" Yukkon asked approaching Hank, handing him a dainty glass of port wine. "Those two boys are most satisfactory, aren't they?"

Hank, accepting the drink, taking sips, the liquid strong enough to tingle his tongue, hated keeping up appearances but knew he had no choice. Not at the moment.

He replied, "They seemed satisfactory to me."

"You're interested in buying them, I take it?"

"I am."

A smile, one that would fit nicely on Satan's face. "Did you get to see them both naked?"

Hank swallowed his mouthful of port, feeling the burn down his throat. "Yeah, I did." He wheezed after that but held his composure.

He hated port.

"That's good." Yukkon nodded. "But tell me, what did you think of them both being uncut?"

Hank wasn't sure where the question was leading, so he decided to remain noncommittal. "I'm not sure, why?"

"No particular reason." Yukkon sipped from his glass, his look turning sinister again momentarily. "But if you prefer your boys to be circumcised, I can arrange the procedure on them before they're delivered to you."

Hank was getting that all too familiar stomach-churning thing happening again—and the strong port wasn't helping matters, either. "That won't be necessary."

"Very well. But if you require *anything* to be done to them, please let me know. I want you to be completely satisfied with your purchase. *Completely* satisfied."

"What do you mean?" And Hank regretted the question as soon as it left his mouth, truly.

Yukkon winked. "If you require them to be branded to mark them as your property for example, that can also be arranged."

"Yeah, I'll have to think about that."

"Naturally." A wicked smirk; the man clearly enjoying talking like this, which made Hank hate him even more. "But if you have *any* request at all, no matter how large or small, please don't hesitate to let me know. A lot of buyers like to alter their purchase according to their particular desires, and I'm happy to do the same for you, George-san."

"Alter them?" It was like they were talking about a pair of jeans, not living breathing humans. Hank now felt his rage, a common feeling in Yukkon's disturbing presence since discovering his operation, that's for sure.

To Hank's further disgust, Yukkon held that awful smile. "Aside from brandings and circumcisions when required, I've also sold boys who've had all their teeth removed, been castrated, or had their tongues taken out. It's all up to you as to how you desire your purchase so that they please you in every way." He then laughed, one that rattled with maliciousness. "I had one buyer who desired a living fleshlight, so they had his boy delivered with his arms and legs amputated. I believe his vocal cords were removed too, from memory. A strange request I know, but it's not for me to judge, only to do as asked."

A bullet into the brain pan was too good for this guy.

Seriously.

At that moment, thank fucking God, a bell chimed to interrupt their macabre conversation. Because yeah, Hank was ready to throw punches at any moment.

An employee of Mister Nakamori's announced, "Please, most honored guests, dinner is served for your pleasure."

Hank then followed a bald-headed man as instructed into the dining room. He was clearly the leader here, even though Yukkon was doing all the talking so far. Hank wanted to talk to him as soon as he could. Find out more about him.

Discover the depth of this gang's ranks, as it were.

But for the here and now, what confronted him when he arrived almost knocked the wind from out of his lungs.

What the actual fucking fuck!

Because there was Tetsu and Rion, lying across the table, both of their heads close to each other, starkers still, and with food—sushi and sashimi mostly—neatly placed all over them.

They were the dinner plates Hank was going to have to eat off of!

"Please be seated and enjoy your meal, our most honored guests," The waiter announced, bowing and then departing without another word.

Hank now witnessed a nantamoiri banquet in all its glory.

Fifth Course

Hank sat cross-legged at the placing he was asked to do so between Yukkon and another man. That man he didn't know, but must have been lower ranking within the gang, because he kept bowing every time another member so much as glanced his way.

Yukkon, however, kept oozing his evil charm, a poisonous fume around him at all times. Hank really needed to kill the fucking bastard. No damn doubt.

"You've used chopsticks before I take it, George-san?" Yukkon asked, picking up his set, clacking them together.

"Yeah, I have." And thank God he had—he enjoyed Asian takeout often. No cooking involved that way, being single mostly. "See?" And to prove it, he picked up his chopsticks and moved them as dexterously as Yukkon had.

"Very good."

From there, and much to Hank's approval considering what was going on, Tetsu and Rion were treated with respect, honor , and complimented often. Given money too. Lots of it. In fact, by the time the meal was mostly done, both Tetsu and Rion's hands were stuffed with cash; some of it placed over their chests because they couldn't hold it all.

So far, this wasn't so bad.

Not until Yukkon announced, "Gentlemen, please do

not eat your last pieces of sushi. There is a special treat for you all tonight, thanks to what our host has arranged for us."

Nods of approval, widening smiles as well, were given.

Hank got a funny feeling in his guts as to where this could lead, preparing himself for anything. Of course, where it did go was nowhere near what he thought, thank fuck. For at that moment, Mister Nakamori entered the dining room carrying a large silver tray.

On the tray, a cup of steaming hot coffee for each guest.

Mister Nakamori served each man in turn according to etiquette, Hank first—being the guest of the host—followed by the bald-headed man, then Yukkon and the rest of them. The lowly man sitting next to Hank was served last.

When Mister Nakamori placed down the last cup, he announced, "Please, honored guests, enjoy your kopi luwak made by wild civets, very rare indeed, while you watch Tetsu-kun and Rion-kun prepare your next delicacy for you."

"Er…what's going on now?" Hank uttered to no one in particular.

But Yukkon, always the talker, the over-explainer, replied, "Normally, the boys provided for our entertainment are masturbated so that we can season our last sushi with their ejaculate." A chuckle, a wink too. "But for tonight, and in your honor, George-san, our host has arranged it so we can obtain the seasoning from Tetsu-kun's anus instead."

Hank was kinda mortified at that, even if he

understood what these sorts of establishments did during their banquets. "I see," he said to reiterate his thoughts.

"Yes, you'll soon see. But I have to say, it's most enjoyable to watch the delicacy we're going to enjoy being prepared."

As if on cue, and after the last pieces of sushi were taken off Tetsu and Rion's bodies, put on proper plates by the waiters and placed by each diner, they then both began doing what was obviously required of them.

Watching Rion come over Tetsu, the look of love in their eyes, Hank suddenly realized the dining room was getting rather warm. Had they turned up the heating? He pulled at the collar of his shirt, wide-eyed as he watched unbelieving what unfolded before him.

It was all so salaciously erotic to watch two fit young men be with each other in such a beautiful way, all lust-filled embraces with trembling, wanting hands, blushing faces, kissing deeply, moans, saliva dripping off tongues, arching backs, muscles taut, and building up a sweat complete with sensual groans and writhing bodies.

Hank got even more flushed when Tetsu not only opened his mouth wider for Rion, but opened his legs for him too, fully receptive and submissive so that his boyfriend could penetrate him.

They embraced each other with greater purpose then, clearly within each other's world, like the audience wasn't even there.

Not at all.

As such, Tetsu was now fully hard and leaking,

stomach quivering, moaning even more, telling Rion he wanted him.

Such a wonderful thing.

Tetsu and Rion, deeply immersed within their passion as well, kissed each other over and over, becoming feverish, panting, grabbing at each other. What a show. The other men watching placed more and more money onto the table, big wads of it, clearly pleased with what they saw. Who could blame them? Hank also reached into his pocket to add whatever money he had, Tetsu and Rion deserving every penny.

Although he noticed Yukkon didn't contribute any funds.

Rion soon gained his rhythm, opening up Tetsu's ass with his thick cock, his perfectly tight round buttocks a beautiful sight to see while he thrust and thrust, rocking the table, glassware clinking. It was also lovely to see his balls, a soft ginger-haired fuzz over them, jiggle in time with his movement too.

Hank was mesmerized.

Tetsu, once Rion was inside him proper, seated as it were, began panting with greater intensity, making wonderful guttural noises from his throat. Rion groaned too, short sharp barks, almost. A chorus. The primal music of their passion.

Their undying love.

"Tetsu-kun and Rion-kun are most pleasing to watch, aren't they?" Yukkon said, nodding.

"They sure are," Hank admitted, aroused and smiling as he realized it.

"You have bought well."

Hank had to shift his weight while sitting cross-legged. He had a hard-on he couldn't believe he had, warm all over, right to his balls as well. It got worse when Rion began thrusting with an even greater fervor, his intensity incredible. The air was electric, full of their passion, clear to everyone they meant so much to one another.

At the same time, Tetsu began yelling his joy, deeper moans from Rion as well. Shudders and eyes tight, clearly enjoying, no needing, the painful bliss of Rion being inside of him.

Nods, claps, and words of approval from the other guests soon overtook everything else. The climax would soon be upon them, Hank knew. They all did.

As expected, Rion then blurted, "I'm gonna cum, baby!"

A growl from Tetsu. "Give it to me!"

Also, and as if a signal, Yukkon sat up, a sort of pipette contraption in his hand; no doubt the thing he'd use to collect what he desired. Where he got it from, Hank couldn't guess. Then again, he imagined the bastard would be prepared for anything.

He also knew he didn't need to know.

Yukkon instructed, "After you've climaxed, Rion-kun, pull out so I can get to the ejaculate you've deposited inside your boyfriend."

Rion didn't answer.

Instead, he responded with many almighty shudders, glassware knocked over that time, a few smashed, as four or five massive jolts resulted when he came inside Tetsu. Hank swore the ground shook, it was that profound. That beautiful and amazing.

The boys shouted their climactic relief too.

A sweet, short moment after that, sweat dripping, panting hard, Rion did as he was asked before moving to Tetsu's side to embrace him lovingly. Gentle kisses were now shared between them.

Hank noticed Tetsu had cum at the same time, his stomach glistening with ribbons of sticky white jizz, right up to his chest. The lower ranking men were mopping it up off Tetsu with their last pieces of sushi before popping them into their mouths, satisfied smiles resulting. More nods and whispers of appreciation followed. More money given too.

"Keep your legs where they are, Tetsu-kun," Yukkon said, "Now gently push out for me so you can open up your anus."

Tetsu did as he was asked.

Again, to witness the two young men together like they had been was something else, especially because it was so amazing. So beautiful. Certainly, something Hank would never forget. Not ever. But to then see Tetsu's asshole, freshly fucked, red and tender looking, bulge and retract as he pushed and pushed, tightening his stomach to reveal his abs, was something else. Truly.

Rion's cum soon oozed from out of Tetsu.

Yukkon began collecting his well paid for prize, an expensive one by the amount of money placed around the boys, that's for sure. Hank felt giddy, but for a completely different reason than before.

He'd gotten really warm. Hard as a rock too. Wowsers.

Hank had to fan his face, everything got that close all of a sudden again.

He tried his best to calm himself.

When Yukkon had collected the jizz that'd trickled out of Tetsu, quite a bit of it really—Rion must have been really horny—he began drizzling it over the bald man's and Hank's sushi. Yukkon did so as if he were a chef on one of those TV cooking shows saucing a meal, with practiced ease and flair. How often did this sort of thing happen at these dinners? What was left in the pipette, Yukkon drizzled onto his own.

"Enjoy, George-san," the bald-headed man said, the first time he'd spoken all evening.

Both men privileged enough to enjoy the "delicacy" from Tetsu because of their status, ate greedily their morsel of sushi, sipping their coffee after that. Both then looked contented.

Hank stared at his.

Yukkon said, "Best to eat it while the ejaculate is still warm, otherwise the taste will be ruined."

Hank, calming himself, picked up the sushi with his chopsticks, not quite sure but not wanting to arouse suspicion, either. He shoved it into his mouth in one go, swallowing without chewing.

Done.

It was true, a tang tasting like really bitter dark chocolate did wash over the back of his tongue. Then again, that could just be how Rion's jizz tasted; Hank wasn't convinced the few moments it was inside Tetsu would have made any difference to its flavor whatsoever.

Okay, there *was* a lemony aftertaste.

Was that what Yukkon referred to which made ejaculate taken from a boy's ass and used as a sushi seasoning a delicacy here? Its citrus aftertaste?

Hank almost laughed, because he knew why that was there; it came from the disinfectant provided by Mister Nakamori. Tetsu clearly had cleaned himself everywhere.

Which, upon thought, was a good thing.

He smiled at that. More so considering he believed the dinner was done now, especially as the coffees were drained and the men started to look restless.

The bald man stood. "It's time to retire to the smoking room, gentlemen."

All stood.

Hank rubbed his legs, not used to sitting cross-legged for so long. He was about to follow the leader out of the dining room like all the others, ducks marching in a row as it were, when Yukkon clapped his hand upon Hank's shoulder.

"Not you, George-san."

Hank's stomach turned uncomfortably. What was going on? Had he aroused too much suspicion? Had he been discovered? What? He didn't feel good now, more so because Tetsu and Rion's future depended on the next few moments.

"Why not?" he managed, putting on the bravest face he could.

Yukkon's glare never left him, even when he clicked his fingers. At that, into the dining room came the four men

Hank immediately recognized from the warehouse, all tats and attitude.

They held guns too.

"These two boys," Yukkon gestured loosely to Tetsu and Rion, who were now up off the table and being held by the men, guns pointed at them ominously, "will be held in my stockroom until you can pay for them in full. That way I can be certain there will be no deception on your part."

"I won't deceive you." Hank replied. "And heck, I can transfer the money to you right now; just give me the bank's details where you want it deposited into, and it'll be done."

Yukkon laughed, almost in Hank's face. "Do you think I'm stupid, George-san?" Man, this bastard had changed his tune now that the pointy end of proceedings was upon them. What an asshole. An evil fucking asshole at that. "No. You will provide the two million in *cash*. When you've withdrawn it, you'll then be instructed as to where it's to be dropped off."

Tetsu and Rion, even though looking scared out of their minds, wisely remained quiet.

Yukkon stepped up to them, running his hand down Tetsu's and Rion's cheeks on turn. "Such pretty boys, aren't you? I wouldn't mind you both for myself."

Tetsu visibly recoiled, as did Rion, before the man added, "But for now, you will both be my *guests* until George-san can pay for you."

Hank, feeling the weight of the situation, said, "It'll take time to get that much money in cash."

"I know."

"Oh."

Yukkon then brushed his attention over Tetsu's cock, grabbing it seconds later. Tetsu yelped. "You will have three days, George-san. After that these boys will go to auction and become fair game for any buyer to purchase, including myself. Is that clear?"

Tetsu looked terrified, eyes wide, glaring at Hank for help, any help, Hank knew. "Fine, Yukkon, you can do that. But can I talk to Tetsu and Rion before you take them away?"

Yukkon nodded. "Very well. But be quick about it." He then let go of Tetsu; the relief from him, Rion, and Hank all too apparent. "Although, if you even think for one moment you can try anything funny, such as attempt any escape with them, you will forfeit your claim on them and I'll have you shot."

Hank nodded.

Fucking hell, he wanted to ram his fist so far down Yukkon's throat he'd only be able to talk out of his ass. No wait. That was too good for him. Hank wanted to rip the bastard's cold heart out and stomp on it.

Yukkon and his goons left the room, as did the waiters. Once the door was closed, Hank raised his hand, letting Tetsu and Rion know that he had to speak first, clearly not much time. "No matter what happens, just trust me, okay?"

Tetsu nodded slowly. "We trust you."

"I do too," Rion added.

Hank moved closer to them. "I'm going to come rescue you, I fucking promise. But first, I've got to organize a few things. Unfortunately, it may take me a couple of days."

"What do we do in the meantime?" Rion asked, voice pained.

Hank replied, "It seems to me Yukkon has taken to you both. Perhaps use that to make your lives a bit easier, but don't do anything that'll put you in danger if you can help it." He rubbed his chin in thought. "And as I've already said, I don't want you to do anything you don't want to, either. But just so you know, I've been to his stockroom where I've seen boys about your age, some younger, kept drugged up and locked in small cages. Trust me even more when I say it's not a place you want to be left in for any amount of time. The conditions there are fucking appalling."

Tetsu looked at Rion; they were holding hands now. "I *think* I've got an idea."

"That's good," Hank replied, hopeful for the first time in a while even though he didn't want to leave Tetsu and Rion. The things he had to do to keep up his disguise sometimes sucked, big time.

Hank wanted to say more, but when Yukkon entered with his four men, beaming a leering smile directed at Tetsu and Rion, clearly their time was up. He hated that man unlike anyone else in his life.

Hated him with a passion.

Much to Tetsu's disappointment, heart heavy, Hank was immediately escorted out of the room, not even able to offer a nod goodbye. Yukkon, the man who was now in charge of what happened to them until Hank could do as promised, began collecting the money that'd been left on the table.

"You've both impressed everyone tonight." He stuffed the massive wad of cash, thousands of dollars at a guess, into his jacket pocket. "But I think you've impressed me most of all."

Now was the moment Tetsu decided to enact his plan, as feeble as it was. "We can impress you even more, sir."

Rion squeezed his hand, giving him the silent "I trust you" sign they now understood between each other.

A raise of eyebrows from Yukkon. "Explain, please."

Tetsu swallowed. "I…I mean, Rion and me…we can be your personal entertainment while you wait for George to pay for us. Instead of sending us to…you know, your stockroom."

"Interesting." Yukkon came closer. "Do tell me more, boy."

Tetsu wasn't sure how to procced; he was certainly at a disadvantage here. Mostly because he really had no idea what a man like Yukkon would consider entertainment.

Tetsu, his mind a muddle as he tried to grapple with his conflicting thoughts, what to think mostly, uttered, "Well…you can watch Rion fuck me as much as you want to. We'll do it for you any time you want, honest."

Rion asked quietly, "What do you say to that, sir?"

"A good start." Yukkon nodded. "But what else are you both willing to do for me to save yourself from the humiliation of being chained, collared and locked in the cages of my stockroom?"

Tetsu didn't know, but became desperate. "What did you want us to do for you?" he asked, regretting that he had, because he'd now left it wide open for Yukkon's full depravity to become apparent.

But much to his surprise, Yukkon simply said, "I do believe your presence in my care will suffice for now. I will have you taken to my summer house for safekeeping. When there, you will be my guests and treated accordingly."

Tetsu was stunned.

"I mean no disrespect, sir," Rion said. "But why would you do that?"

Yukkon now smiled, an evil, cruel and ugly-looking grimace across his insipid features. "Because I know that your buyer isn't who he says he is, and that the both of you will be the insurance I need until I find out more."

Stunned, Tetsu asked, "Are we your hostages, then?"

"We shall see. But rest assured, whatever capacity you find yourselves in within my care, you will be treated well." Yukkon clicked his fingers again; Mister Nakamori rushed into the dining room. "Because if by some slim chance George-san is who he says he is, then I don't want you damaged in any way before he pays for you both."

Tetsu was speechless; his worry now for Hank, not himself.

To Mister Nakamori, Yukkon said, "Return their clothing to them. Oh, and give them this..." From his jacket he produced the bundle of money, handing it to the restaurant's owner. "Also pay them what you promised them for their work here tonight."

Mister Nakamori bowed low, almost to the ground. "As you please, it shall be done, Yukkon-sama."

"I then want you to organize it for them to be escorted to my *summer house* as discretely and securely as you can."

Tetsu suddenly didn't like how Yukkon said "summer house" like it was some sort of code for something else. Something sinister. He gulped, but remained silent.

A glinting, knowing look from Mister Nakamori toward Tetsu and Rion. "It shall be done, Yukkon-sama."

"But do stay for a moment." Yukkon then retrieved his phone from another pocket while Mister Nakamori bowed obediently. When whoever he'd dialled answered, Yukkon said coldly, "Ah, Joe-san. So nice to hear your voice once more. How are you, my old friend?"

Tetsu couldn't hear the reply.

What Yukkon said next gave him a big clue. "I heard your adorable and rather tasty nephew Mason was seen with the real estate tycoon George Riewoldt at *Badda-Bings* the other night. Is this true?"

A response, again no guesses as to what it was.

"Yes, George Riewoldt is his name." A look of impatience crossed Yukkon's face. "You know of him, surely. He *was* seen entering your apartment not long before he contacted me."

A long pause.

"I see."

Another long pause.

"It seems to me I've chosen the correct course of action, then. Thank you for your assistance once more, Joe-san. I do hope you enjoyed the blowjob you received from that cop. It'll be the last he'll give you."

Tetsu's stomach flipped in fear. Shit! Hank had been found out!

Rion sucked in a deep breath.

Yukkon turned to them, a smile so cruel upon his face it frightened Tetsu. "Looks like you'll both will be my hostages, after all."

Sixth Course

Hank sat in his car for ages after being escorted out of the restaurant, fuming that he couldn't do anything to get Tetsu and Rion out of there. He hated how he felt so ineffectual, how this alternate persona he needed to be to do his job had created such weakness in him.

He'd much rather rush in and bust heads. He knew he couldn't do that, there was Tetsu and Rion's safety to consider right now. Because if there was one thing Hank knew to his core, Yukkon would kill them without so much a blink if he suspected anything amiss.

Or do something worse...

Then he started the engine, deciding to head home and suck down a couple of bottles of booze, his phone rang, connecting to his car's Bluetooth immediately.

"Hey there, Hank. Joe here."

"Fuck!" Joe was the last person Hank would have thought he'd hear from, especially considering the circumstances and his predicament because of him. "What do *you* want?"

He already hated the conversation and the memories churned up after hearing the man's voice, tasting Joe's disgustingly bitter jizz in his mouth again, wincing as he did so.

"I've got information you'll wanna hear."

"Spit it out, then." Just then, Hank wished he'd spat not swallowed; he swore Joe's jizz was still making itself known down there in his guts somewhere.

He shivered uncomfortably.

A shuffle, a moment of pause, before Joe, his voice distressed, blurted, "Yukkon knows you're a cop."

"Fucking what?" Hank almost swerved off the road, hitting one of those bollards that seemed to be sprinkled everywhere like forest mushrooms in this part of the city. His heart skipped beats too. "How the fuck did he find that—oh, wait? You told him, didn't you, you fucking bastard?"

"I had no choice."

"Really?" Hank turned the car forcefully, seatbelt tightening, tires squealing, as he headed back toward the restaurant, a panic overtaking him to make him sweat.

Tetsu and Rion needed him. Now *was* the time to bust heads, seeing as his cover was blown all thanks to blabber fucking mouth Joe. Why Hank ever trusted the man was beyond him. Honestly.

"Yeah, really."

"Well, Joe, thanks for nothing, fucker."

Silence from Joe as Hank pushed down hard on the accelerator, engine screaming as he sped on, his heart racing too as he realized one thing. He probably didn't have much time.

When Joe finally did speak, his words shocked Hank more than they already had. "I'm worse than you know. It's because of me Yukkon is going to kill Mason, Hank."

Hank slammed on the brakes.

A moment of stunned silence, breathing hard, before he asked, "What's Mason got to do with all this?"

"Do you know why I knew where he worked?"

"I'm sure you're going to tell me."

"Mason…he's my nephew."

Hank's head spun and everything came crashing in around him. He was speechless. Beyond stunned. How could such a beautiful boy, precious and wonderful, be related to such a monster? Life sure knew how to throw curve balls, didn't it?

Hank mouthed words for a moment to reply, but no sound eventuated.

"Hello? You still there, Hank?"

Hank sucked in a breath, steeling his resolve as best he could. "You've fucked up big time, haven't you, Joe?"

"I have." A pause, one longer than waiting for water to boil, it seemed. "But you've got to get Mason to safety before it's too late. If it's not already too late. Yukkon doesn't delay when it comes to such things."

Hank wanted to choke the life out of Joe with his bare hands for this.

Instead, he did the only thing he could do. "Fuck! Fucking! Fuck!" he cursed over and over again, hitting the steering wheel with bunched fists, car shaking as a result, realizing all too clearly his dilemma now.

Because no matter what choice he made, they would both be wrong. If he went to get Mason, Tetsu and Rion could be harmed; and if he went to Tetsu and Rion, Mason could be.

Hank spat, "You've really put me in one very difficult fucking situation you know that, you bastard."

"I'm sorry."

"Like fuck you are."

"I'm being honest here. I didn't want...Mason..." Joe was clearly distressed. Good. But when Hank calmed enough, needing to, Joe seemed to be sobbing, his voice stilted and emotion-filled as well. "Please, Hank. Go s-save...go help m-my nephew. *Please.*" Joe hung up.

"You fucker, you could of at least told me his address before you left me hanging like this," Hank said to no one now. He then asked his car to dial Joe. No answer. He did it one more time. Nothing. "You *really* do piss me off!"

Hank, however, decided Mason was in more immediate danger. And the only reasoning he could come up with for that was the fact Yukkon had seemed to take a liking to Tetsu and Rion. Enough of a liking to keep them alive until he could get to them.

He hoped.

Hank turned the car around, more squealing tires, heading for the flower shop, the only place he could think of to go. It was late, past 9:00 pm. Would Mason even be there?

He'd soon find out, he reckoned.

When the shop came into view, a light was on inside. Hank, holding onto hope, parked out front, jumped out of the car, and dashed for the shop's front door, banging on it loudly.

He saw movement. There *was* someone in there.

Hank knocked again.

"All right, all right, keep your pants on. I'm coming!" Mason called, Hank both relieved he was there *and* alive.

When the boy came into view through the glass door, Hank's heart skipped a beat, wonderfully so. Mason was achingly good-looking, to Hank anyway, and he then realized how much he needed him in his life.

Needed him so much.

Mason, obviously recognizing Hank, eyebrows raised, also looked puzzled but opened the door after unlocking it anyway. "What are you doing here?" A study of Hank for a moment with a small smile forming in the corner of his lips...if Hank wasn't mistaken. "And how did you know I worked here?"

Hank, trying to remain nonchalant even though his insides flipped and his heart thumped, replied, "I'm a cop. Also, your uncle Joe told me to come get you because you're in danger."

Mason blinked.

Hank reiterated, "You're in danger, Mason. Real danger. So please, you've got to come with me right now. Okay?"

Mason, still looking stunned, nodded slowly, clearly accepting what Hank told him. He closed the shop's door and locked it after he stepped into the street next to Hank.

"Then...let's go already," the boy said, his nervousness apparent though his voice.

Before Hank knew it, Mason was in his car. All lovely floral aromas pervaded everything; they were clearly from the shop. Underneath that though, was Mason's more wood-scented cologne. Very intoxicating. Hank had to do his best to concentrate on the road ahead.

After a time, Mason simply stated, "I don't know your name."

"Hank. Hank Riley. That's my name."

A nod. Then another long moment of studied silence, Mason clearly processing things. Hank couldn't blame him. This whole situation, from that night at *Badda-Bings* to right now, was one hell of a roller-coaster ride.

No fucking doubt about it.

When Hank turned off onto the on-ramp of the freeway, heading north, Mason said, "You hurt me, you know that, Hank."

Hank shifted his weight within his car's seat, wanting to reach over and hold Mason's hand but forcing himself to not do so. Not yet. "I'm sorry. It's just that being with you…that was the first time I'd ever been with another guy. And as lame as it sounds, I was scared. So scared. But…in those moments you were with me, you changed my life for the better, Mason. You really did."

An intake of breath. "I did?"

"You did, Mason. I also realize now that I need you. I need you for who you are and for what you make me. So please, trust me when I say I won't ever leave you hanging ever again."

Mason's eyes went all watery, his bottom lip quivering. "You…*need* me? Like, as in me being your boyfriend need?"

"Yeah, *that* kind of need."

Hank, putting the car into cruise control while on the freeway, the road relatively quiet, gave himself a moment to really look at Mason. He *was* beautiful. Even more so with the overhead lighting bathing him in an orange glow, his golden hair more beautiful than a chocolate box sunset. So angelic. Stunningly so. It was then Hank realized he meant every word.

"I see."

"I know that all sounds lame," Hank admitted, "but there it is. The truth."

Mason's expression turned dark, tainting his glow. "So…um, let me get this straight. You let me seduce you so I'd suck your dick, then when I wanted it to go further you bailed like a chicken shit married man with a guilty conscience." His eyes narrowed. "And then, to top it all off, I don't hear a word from you for days, not even a text message, and now you show up claiming you need me and you're here to rescue me, like I'm some damsel in distress. I've got a news flash for you, Hank. You're no knight in shining armor."

Hank felt a terrible lump form in his throat, because the boy was right. When he'd swallowed it down enough, his heart still thumping, he said, "I deserved that."

"Oh, you deserve a lot more."

"I get that too. I was a jerk." Hank looked at Mason once more, right into those bluest blues of his. "But can we…start over?"

Mason folded his arms. "I want to see Uncle Joe first. You need to know a few things before anything else happens between us."

Hank, not believing that was the best course of action above all else, reluctantly said, "Fine. But I don't think—"

"At the moment I don't want to know what you think," Mason interrupted. "So please, just do as I've asked of you. All right?"

Hank made a U-turn when he could.

From there, they drove back into the city in silence. Mason kept his attention out the window. Hank, unable to think otherwise, knew he'd blown it with the boy.

And that hurt him.

When parked in the underground carpark beneath Joe's apartment, Mason finally spoke. "Thanks for bringing me here."

Hank believed he caught another glimpse of a smile then.

"Don't mention it." Hank though, had to ask, "I don't mean any offence when I say this, but you do know your uncle is one of the evillest men I've ever had the displeasure of meeting, don't you?"

"You're wrong about him."

Hank harrumphed. "Funny how family members always say that until it's too late."

"Whatever. You'll soon find out."

Hank didn't want to get into an argument, not before they were boyfriends, anyway; because if he was reading the signs right, Mason *was* interested in that. Those little smiles. The sideways looks. And besides, it was only after the actual fucking began that disagreements became inevitable, so there was plenty of time yet.

Heck, he'd had some doozies with Judy.

And to tell the truth, even though it was never planned or sought out—Hank wasn't a jerk in *that* way—makeup sex was pretty darn good. Until such a thing eventuated, knowing there needed to be a relationship first as well, he had to be on his best behavior.

He didn't want to lose Mason now.

All the way to Joe's apartment, Hank tried to think of something to say to Mason which would smooth the waters he'd clearly disturbed. Let him know he truly was sorry for what he'd done as well. Unfortunately, he couldn't think of anything, simply feeling out of his depth.

Hank knocked on Joe's door.

As soon as it was opened, Joe blurted, "I told you not to come here again, Hank."

"Well, here I fucking am. Deal with it."

Joe, with increased venom but also looking worried, spat, "I'm being watched by every fucker imaginable here. Gimme a break. You're putting all of us in danger, you bloody idiot."

"It's okay, Uncle Joe." From behind Hank, Mason came. "Hank came and got me as you asked him to. I'm safe."

Joe's face brightened.

A split second later, the both of them were in an embrace. "Oh, my dear boy, I'm so glad you're all right. So glad, it warms my heart."

"Me too."

From there, Joe invited them in. And if what the man had told them earlier, which Hank didn't doubt he'd lie about such a thing—not when his family was involved—this wasn't going to be a long conversation. He needed to get Mason away from here asap.

But Hank had to know one thing. "You're a lying, double-crossing, fucking bastard, aren't you, Joe?"

Mason glared at Hank.

Joe smiled. "Oh, I'm far worse than that."

Now it was Mason's turn to say something. "You don't have to tell him anything, Uncle Joe. But if you do, that's the reason I brought him here. So, he knows."

"Tell me what?" Hank questioned.

Joe shrugged, "That my lies are far deeper than what even you can imagine, Hank."

Hank looked between them both. "And I suppose you're now going to tell me you're not a murdering, corpse fucking bastard, either."

Joe laughed, but also looked saddened. "I'm not, no."

"What?" Hank realized Joe wasn't lying, the conviction in his eyes clear. Blue eyes. Not as bright as Mason's, but the family resemblance was striking. "But hang on, wasn't your jizz found in that boy's anal cavity, the autopsy stating he'd been fucked hours after his death?"

Mason remained by his uncle's side. He had also hooked his arm within Joe's, his head resting on his shoulder too. The love between them was clear.

What exactly was going on here?

Suddenly, and as if the weight he'd been bearing for so long had finally crushed him because Mason was here with him, supporting him, tears fell from Joe's eyes. "He was so beautiful, that precious boy. My precious Shin. So beautiful."

Hank was taken aback. "What?"

Joe looked to Mason. Mason gave him a nod,

permission to continue, as it were. The result could have knocked Hank over with a feather what was said after that.

"I loved Shin so, so much," Joe began. "I still do. He was my everything. And they…they took that away from me all because I wanted out. Because I wanted for nothing else but to spend my life with Shin in peace."

And that's when it hit Hank. "You…you didn't kill him. You didn't even fuck him after he was…dead, did you?"

Joe was bawling now, shoulders heaving, Mason comforting him, cradling his head. "It's okay, let it all out, Uncle Joe."

When Joe did so, recovering enough, his face wet, he mumbled, "The last time I saw him, there were rope and cigarette burns all over his body where they'd strung him up and tortured him all because of me. They'd raped and defiled him over and over and over again. They didn't care about him. They…they were the ones who killed him because of what they did to him. Not me. Not me at all. I'd never."

Hank felt the room spin, his stomach queasy. "I'm… sorry."

Joe's resolve seemed to steel, and with spittle flying and tears still flowing, eyes red-rimmed, lips quivering with anger, he roared, "I had to get the gang back for what they did to my Shin. I *had* to make them pay. To do that I had to…I had to set it up to look like I'd committed the worst crime possible against my most beautiful boy. All to get them to trust me again. Trust me enough so I that could exact my revenge against them all."

"Dear God!"

Joe, the floodgates opened, continued, "I still have nightmares to this day about what I did. I loved Shin. I loved him so much. But…suffice it to say, from there I played the part of the evil necrophiliac you were all too happy to accept so I could do what I had to do. Become an informant to put them all away one by one—it worked for that prick Mister Yaketsuku, didn't it?"

Hank now had to admire Joe, even if his chosen path wasn't exactly the right one. "You delightfully sneaky fucking bastard, you."

Joe looked at Hank, right in his eyes again, the truth remaining within them clear beyond the pain he'd obviously relived. "I'd have never hurt Shin. Not anyone, really. I only did what I had to do."

"I believe you."

Joe wiped his face. "I've been found out, which is why they're now after the only one left I love. You know what you have to do, Hank. So do it. Rid me and everyone else of this nightmare."

Mason hugged his uncle.

Hank sucked in a breath. "I've got to get Yukkon and all the rest of them."

"Yes."

Hank knew what he had to do next. "Then let's go, Mason."

Mason stood, hugging then kissing his uncle on his forehead before saying goodbye. "I'll see you soon, Uncle Joe."

"I hope so," Joe replied.

As they were leaving Joe's apparently "not-so-protected" apartment, Hank turned to the man he now respected—such a fucking surprise that. "So…you wanting Jake's jizzed on underwear for information before I…you know, did what I did for you…that was all part of your act, right?"

Joe smiled. "That, you'll never know."

Hank harrumphed. "You know, I still hate you."

"And I hate you."

Hank smiled now, patting Joe on his shoulder. "See you soon, Joe."

"I look forward to that moment with baited breath."

Hank laughed.

But clearly the conversation wasn't over, because Mason, smiling, cheekily, chimed in, "Um…what exactly *did* you do for Uncle Joe, Hank?"

Before Hank could answer, Joe said, "Oh, he sucked my cock for information on Yukkon's whereabouts."

Mason gasped. "Oh, is that right? You went down on my uncle but you didn't want to fuck me when I begged for it?" Hank was at a loss for a moment, flushing with heated embarrassment too, until Mason, that corner lipped smile of his wider, added, "But I *suppose* I could give you another opportunity."

"What?"

Mason giggled. "Another opportunity to fuck me, of course."

Hank now blinked, disbelieving what had transpired. "Are you saying you want to be my boyfriend?"

"Yes, silly, I'm saying just that."

Tetsu and Rion were driven by Mister Nakamori out of the city and into the national forests. They'd had their hands and feet bound by rope, expertly knotted, the both of them in the back seat of the car, as far away from each other as possible.

To further prevent any escape, they were also fitted with collars and chains which were then secured to the car's booster seat loops with padlocks.

Clearly, this was Yukkon's idea of making sure they were secure.

Although, the farther they went into the depths of the forest, Tetsu began to fear even more for his life. He was scared unlike any other time, because he got the feeling "going to the summer house" didn't mean spending a lovely weekend in a log cabin in front of an open fireplace snuggling up with Rion.

To make matters worse, Rion looked scared out of his mind, something that scared him even more. If his strength and support was like that, what hope did Tetsu have? None. Still, he held an ember of it within him. Mostly because he believed Hank would find them. He had to find them, right?

"Where are you taking us?" Tetsu asked, his voice shaking as much as he did.

Mister Nakamori snorted. "Somewhere you won't return from."

At least that answered one question: they *were* going to be killed.

"Why are you doing this?" Tetsu had to ask, seeing no other reason not to.

"Because I do as I'm told."

"You don't have to, you know that, Mister Nakamori."

The man snorted again. "Are you now going to offer yourselves to me to try and make me change my mind?"

Rion piped up, "If that is what it takes, yeah."

"Don't make me laugh…" But a considered pause from the man while he drove on into the forest, the world around them without any city lighting suddenly as dark as how Tetsu felt. "But perhaps I *could* have some fun with you both before I make you dig your own graves, yes."

Tetsu, sensing an opportunity, said, "We could make you happy for a very long time, Mister Nakamori—if you spared our lives."

A lick of lips. A shift of weight. "You'd give yourselves to me willingly whenever I wanted it?"

Tetsu looked at Rion. An *I trust you* was mouthed by his boyfriend, giving him the strength to say, "We would."

Mister Nakamori pulled his car over to the side of the road, stopping before he went up an embankment. He breathed in deeply. "You are most handsome, the both of you."

"I'm glad you think so," Rion said.

"But…I don't desire you."

Tetsu's heart skipped a beat, things suddenly derailing as far as he was concerned. Desperately, he said, "We can make you desire us."

"Yeah, we can do that," Rion said. "We can do anything you want us to do for you, Mister Nakamori."

"Call me Kane."

Tetsu began to feel the oppressive weight of the situation.

He looked at Rion with all his love, his emotions beginning to get the better of him, hiccupping, feeling deep sadness, scared again, before adding. "Please, we don't want to die, *Kane*."

"We all die, Tetsu-kun."

Mister Nakamori undid his seatbelt and got out of his car, going to Tetsu's side of it. Seconds later, he opened the door, one of the restaurant's kitchen knives suddenly appearing with a dextrous flick of his wrist into his hand, gripped tight, knuckles white.

The faint light from the skies above, no doubt moonlight filtering through the canopy, caught the blade's edge. A glint. One of doom, as far as Tetsu was concerned.

"*Please*, we'll do anything," Tetsu begged, feeling tears burn his eyes, his stomach tighten terribly because of his state of panic too. "*Please*."

Mister Nakamori's expression softened; he lowered his hand, looking defeated all of a sudden. "Then would you kill me if I asked such a thing from you?"

Tetsu was taken aback, unbelievably so. At the same time, he also wasn't sure. Was this man, this sick and twisted individual who'd procured young men for a sex slave syndicate for God knows how many years, playing with him or was he serious? He believed the former. No doubt about it.

"I don't understand?" Tetsu said, hearing Rion's surprise too.

"Do you think I wanted to do the things I did? Do you think I had a choice? No. There is no choice when it comes to Mister Yaketsuku or any of his men, Yukkon included. No choice at all. There is only blind obedience."

"What...what happens now?" Rion asked.

Mister Nakamori leaned down, cutting the rope binding Tetsu's hands and feet. He then unlocked the collar. Tetsu was freed. He still couldn't believe what'd happened. No way.

But before he could think about what had transpired, process it all, Mister Nakamori offered Tetsu the knife.

With an expression as close to happiness as Tetsu had ever seen on him, he said, "Now do as I've asked you, Tetsu-kun. End my misery. Stop the nightmares I have each and every night because I can remember all of the faces of all of those boys I've sent into sexual slavery. The boys I've ultimately murdered as if by my own hands."

Tetsu looked down at the knife, more than tempted. "There must be another way."

"There is no other way," he snapped impatiently...until his shoulders slumped; a pleading look then found the man. "It is either I kill you both and then continue my evil with no choice but to obey, or you kill me and finish this. It's all in your hands, yes. You said you'd so anything. So do this. Run the knife I've offered you through me. End it."

Rion asked, "Um...won't they hunt us knowing we've killed you, then?"

"Oh, God, you're right!" Mister Nakamori's mouth

dropped open and he fell to his knees. "You're right. There is no escape for me. If you kill me, they'll look for you. If I kill myself, the same thing. It's impossible. I'm doomed until the end of my days to wear the filthy stain of what I've done. Doomed."

Tetsu was thoughtful. "There *is* another option."

Rion shot Tetsu a quizzical look. "What are you thinking, baby?"

Tetsu wasn't sure, not completely, but he had to say what was festering within his mind, still immature, but needing to be said for everyone's sake. Because the options presented so far weren't good.

"Do go on," Mister Nakamori said, looking up.

Tetsu wanted their safety guaranteed first. "Let me free Rion, and I'll tell you."

A bow of his head in agreeance.

Tetsu didn't waste any time. He got to it, cutting the ropes and unlocking Rion from his collar and chain. When they were both truly freed, Tetsu, feeling that small glimmer of hope ignite further within him because they weren't meeting their maker tonight, returned his attention to Mister Nakamori.

The man, handsome really, slick black hair, ribbon tied, short in stature but also imposing, wearing expensive clothing—a traditional Yokosuka jacket made of silk and embroidered expertly with a detailed dragon on the back—was now standing, staring up at the branches swaying gently in a breeze. It was like he was meditating.

Or, more than likely, waiting for Tetsu's idea to save them all.

Tetsu and Rion got out of the car, both holding hands immediately. Together, they approached Mister Nakamori.

Tetsu, more an observation than anything else, asked, "You've got some wicked knife skills, haven't you?"

Mister Nakamori turned to face them, shrugging. "I run a restaurant."

Tetsu obviously wanted to say he knew that, but chose to proceed with his idea. "Then why don't you fight them? Why don't you go and make a difference for all of the boys that'll be in danger from now on because men like Yukkon exist? Why don't you start by...protecting us with your skills?"

A blank stare, then a burst of laughter. "My, my you seriously think one man, and a man like me no less, can oppose them? Or for that matter, that a man like me can protect you both from them?"

"Hank is opposing them and trying to protect as many as he can in the process," Rion interjected. "If he can do it, why can't you?"

Another moment of pause. "He's a cop."

"And you're a man who knows the underworld inside out, every member, all their hideouts, their plans, their secrets too. To add to that, you've also got ninja-like knife skills," Tetsu said. "You could be an assassin, truly."

"Because of the beauty of youth still blessing you, you're a true romantic, aren't you, Tetsu-kun? It's quite charming, really."

"I'm more an optimist."

Another derisive snort from Mister Nakamori. "The glass isn't half full here."

Rion, squeezing Tetsu's hand, asked, "Then what do you suggest we do, 'cause no one's killing no one here tonight, got it?"

Tetsu loved how brave his boyfriend sounded, even though only moments ago they were both almost releasing their bladders in fear. An amazing change in their circumstances, for sure. Fortunate too, really.

"I can never rid myself of the stain of what I've done," Mister Nakamori stated. "Nor can I ever clean away all that blood, no matter what I do with every breath I breathe from now on."

"You can," Tetsu said, "honest."

"Is that so?" Another huff. "You don't know the depths of my evil, all because I wanted to line my pockets by obeying blindly the men paying me to do their bidding." Mister Nakamori's eyes began to water, his shoulders shuddering. "I've arranged for boys, handsome and fit and in the prime of their lives, to be drugged and then mutilated in an underground surgery. I did that because I was paid handsomely by the buyer who didn't like something about the boy they'd purchased or they had a particular fetish they wanted realized."

Rion swayed, like he was going to faint.

Tetsu held onto him even more. "You did evil things, that's not in question here. But you can do good from now on. Right?"

A huff. "What good is doing good when I have such things on my conscience? I've heard the screams as backyard surgeons hacked away body parts from a boy without using any proper anaesthetics. These screams can never be silenced. You have no idea what it does to a man knowing he was responsible for such despicable acts against another person."

Tears fell, but were they crocodile ones?

Tetsu believed they were genuine. Well...he hoped they were. He let go of Rion to grab Mister Nakamori's hand; it was cold. "Many people have done terrible things all because they're scared."

"I wasn't scared, I was greedy."

But it was then he saw something in Mister Nakamori's dark eyes; and because of that, his idea, already emerging, spoken in part already, solidified even more in his thoughts. "I also know of people who have done terrible things because they haven't known love."

A sharp breath, a disbelieving glare after looking down at the hand that held his. "I beg your pardon?"

Tetsu smiled. "After a time, and caught in your own web as you said, you eventually believed you'd never find anyone who'd love you as much as you knew you could love them. Am I right, Kane?"

At that, Mister Nakamori fell to his knees again, defeated it seemed, Tetsu having no choice but to let him go as the man held his hands to his face, hiding himself. "I don't deserve to be loved."

Rion said, "You're right, you don't. But does that stop you from trying to redeem yourself so that one day someone *might* love you?"

The man looked up, tears running down his face. "You think anyone would ever love a monster like me?"

"I can't answer that," Tetsu admitted honestly.

Rion added, "But actions speak louder than words. So why don't you start acting like you want to make a difference instead of being a mindless puppet? Why don't you protect me and Tetsu right now and get us back into the city safely?"

"I will be killed the moment they know I'm no longer with them."

"Ask Hank for help, then," Tetsu suggested.

Mister Nakamori laughed. "What makes you think he'll want to help me?"

Tetsu held his smile, sensing victory. "He'll help you because I'll tell him to help you, that's why."

A look between them both. "You'd do such a thing for me?"

Rion said, "A funny feeling, someone helping you, isn't it? Feels kinda nice, don't it?"

Mister Nakamori bowed, face almost to the leaf strewn ground. "Then I will protect you and get you to where you want to go safely, my word is my honor, Tetsu-kun and Rion-kun, I assure you. From there, I'll go to Hank and face my fate, whatever it shall be."

Tetsu bowed back, knowing Mister Nakamori's fate would be a jail sentence. "Thank you."

And that "thank you" wasn't for the man himself. No. It was because—and as if by some miracle—his plan had worked. He'd talked Mister Nakamori into changing his mind.

Seventh Course

When within the relative safety of his own home after being dropped off by Mister Nakamori, relieved beyond words he was, Tetsu lay with Rion on their bed, sinking into it, holding his hand and enjoying the silence no longer punctuated by fear. Tetsu, to be honest, felt shattered because of everything that'd happened since first going to *Dankon no yorokobi*, but was glad he was alive. Glad he was with Rion too.

Very glad.

"Do you think he'll change?" Rion asked.

"I don't know." And that was as honest an answer as he could give.

Could a leopard change his spots, or whatever the saying was? Tetsu hoped so, but for that he didn't hold out much hope. Money was the root of all evil, for sure. And to him, Mister Nakamori worshipped that above all else.

"At least he didn't kill us," Rion said, knocking Tetsu from his reverie.

Tetsu then felt guilt prickle at him, not sure why until he said, "You know, if he didn't accept my idea, I would have used that knife to kill him like he wanted me to."

Rion sat up, looking at Tetsu with a surprised expression. "Would you have really?"

"To stay with you, yes I would have."

"Oh, God...I love you!" Rion crashed his lips against Tetsu's.

"I love you too," Tetsu said breathless and aroused when they parted, feeling as close to Rion as he'd ever felt.

From there, they both shed their clothing and became entwined, deeply so. As one, Rion fucked Tetsu unlike any other time before, so full of love and joy and passion, it was incredible.

Toe curling, mind blowing, wonderfully incredible.

No lie.

When done, the both of them spent because they'd shared so much passion, Tetsu held Rion so he could hear his boyfriend's still rapid heartbeat while he cooled, while they both did.

"I don't want to share our intimate experiences with anyone else ever again," Tetsu admitted. "It's just you and me from now on. Okay?"

"I hear that."

"I'm glad you do." And Tetsu was, no doubt. He never wanted to be naked in front of anyone else other that Rion again. Not ever. "Say, how about tomorrow we start looking for an apartment together? Seeing as Mister Nakamori gave us all the money for what we did today."

"I think that's a great idea."

Tetsu then had another thought. "But I think I'd better call Hank to let him know we're all right. He'll worry otherwise."

"Good idea." Rion ran his hand over Tetsu's back. "And after that, can I fuck you again?"

"Oh, you'll be fucking me three more times at least before we go to sleep tonight."

"I'll hold you to that."

Tetsu smiled when he saw Rion's hard-on already at attention, leaking dew drops of pre-cum in anticipation of what would happen next. He was going to be sore tomorrow.

And that was a good thing…

From Joe's, Hank drove to his apartment, believing it as safe as any place for Mason right now. He lived in a secure building. Although, being doubly cautious, he decided to take the less direct route through the city to get there, ensuring no one was following him.

No one seemed to be.

During the journey, enjoying how Mason had seemed to accept him, his hand kept on Hank's thigh while he drove, a touch that was both warm and lovely, he called Chief Inspector Schellenberger.

"Sorry to disturb you so late, Chief."

"No problem—but I'm sure zhis isn't a social call, Inspector Riley?"

Hank had been keeping his boss up-to-date on the situation; he therefore understood events up until now, including how Tetsu and Rion were both safe and sound. Mason too. It was only a matter of rescuing all those other boys—and even though they might be nameless, they were no less important.

"No, it's not," Hank replied. "We will have to act

quickly to get Yukkon and his men from doing any more harm—I don't think they'll hesitate to go to ground, either."

"Do you fear for zhe lives of zhe other boyz he's holding captive?"

"I do."

"Zhen you have my support and permission to organize a dawn raid on zhat warehouse. Use all zhe resources you need to do vhat you have to. Good night, Inspector Riley."

"G'nite, boss."

As soon as the phone was hung up, Mason said, "Your voice goes all sexy when you talk like a cop, you know that?" To emphasize his words, the boy moved so that his hand was closer to Hank's groin.

Closer to his sudden bulge too.

"Does it now?"

"It does."

Mason brushed his attention over Hank's hardness, making Hank suck in a breath through his teeth, shivering with delight. He wanted nothing else now than for his cock to be freed of its cloth prison so that the boy could give it his proper attention.

Mason added, "But do you know what would be even sexier?"

Hank gulped, feeling light headed along with everything aching inside him now, right down to his balls, wonderfully so. "What w-would be...even sexier?"

A lust-filled and eager grin, right to Mason's blues. "If you pull over right now, handcuff me in a mock arrest, spread me over the bonnet of your car, then fuck my ass until you cum deep inside me to make me officially your boyfriend. *That* would make it sexier."

"Holy fuck!" Hank almost creamed in his undies there and then.

And before Hank knew it, he'd parked in his private car parking space underneath his apartment, reaching over to the glove box to retrieve his handcuffs, his hands trembling with both nervousness and anticipation.

Mason, getting into his role already, turning Hank on even more because of it, said seductively, "I've been a bad boy, officer. Very bad. What are you going to do about that, huh?"

Fuck, being with a guy sure was different already.

And that's not to say straight couples didn't role play, of course they did, but this was a first for Hank. "I'm going to arrest your fucking tight little ass, that's what I'm going to do, boy."

"Oh, yeah." Mason was squirming in his seat, leather creaking, licking his lips too, clearly turned on. "*Then* what are you going to do to me?"

Hank, getting it, replied, "Let me fucking show you instead of just gabbing on about it." And with that he got out of the car, rushing to the passenger's side.

Forcefully he opened the door, his arousal-fuelled impatience more than evident. He then grabbed Mason by his arm to pull him out of the car; he'd never do that with a real criminal, but this was all an act. One that turned him on unbelievably.

Mason, his cheeks reddened with large roses, eyes

dilated, let Hank manhandle him. "I'm innocent, officer, I swear it. It wasn't me."

"It *was* you who did it, you fucking little liar." He hoped he hadn't come on too strong with that line. "So now you're under arrest."

Mason moaned, clearly enjoying how Hank was playing along. "Aren't you going to read me my rights first?"

Hank, after handcuffing Mason's hands behind his back, pushed the boy down onto his knees, unzipping to free his raging hard on. "You only have the right to suck my fucking cock to get it all nice and wet for what's going to happen to you next."

"Yes, officer."

Hank, knowing why, because it was one of his fantasies too, feeling empowered and more confident now thanks to Mason, ordered, "Call me daddy, boy."

A flash of confusion over Mason's flushed, wanting expression for a moment. "Yes...officer *daddy*."

Hank, even though he realized that sounded kinda cheesy, admitted he liked the addition. "Jeez, that's damn fucking sexy, boy."

From there, Hank thrust his throbbing, aching cock into Mason's wet, warm mouth. And just like how he'd done that night at *Badda-Bings*, the boy sucked on Hank with eagerness, dripping saliva, gagging sounds, and so much passion it made Hank almost burst, it really did.

It was incredible.

Even better than Hank remembered.

But he decided to keep up with what Mason desired as

his fantasy, play the role even more by being in charge. "Look up at me when you're sucking my cock, boy."

Mason did so without hesitation, his eyes watery and lust-filled. He also slurped, licked, and sucked on Hank's cock like a good and obedient boy, writhing and breathing hard through his nose as he did so, nostrils flared. Mason really was eagerly getting into what he did. So much so, tears of his lust fell down his cheeks along with his saliva, which then dripped onto the concrete between his legs in big drizzling threads. More moaning, deep from his throat to make Hank's cock vibrate. Very fucking hot to feel, for sure.

Again, he'd felt nothing like it.

Because of that, Hank was soon close to climax. He had to hold on though. He knew he had to give Mason what he desired before he came; the boy deserved to be fucked. And Hank wouldn't chicken out this time, no fucking way.

As such, he pulled Mason up to his feet. "You have the right to remain silent while I fuck you." Hank then kissed him, deeply and with his tongue exploring the new wonder that was now his. When parted, almost breathless because their kiss was that good, he added, "But whatever you do say will be used in the bedroom from now on to really get you horny for me."

Mason nodded. "Please fuck me, officer daddy," he pleaded, lips trembling.

"Too bloody right."

Hank pushed Mason face down onto the bonnet of his car, making sure before he spread his legs that he'd yanked down his jeans and underwear to reveal his beautiful rounded buttocks, white and perfect. He gulped at the wonder of them, nicely covered in a soft fuzz of blond/white hair.

Mason kept squirming in delight, the chain of the handcuffs clinking, drippling saliva as much as his precum onto the paintwork of Hank's car in equal measure. The boy was panting for it, and that was one of the most erotic things Hank had ever seen.

Drove him wild, in fact.

After opening Mason's legs wider, really spreading them to open him up, the sight of the back of the boy's pinkish balls, plump and very grabble, he realized that was nothing compared to what his puckered hole looked like.

Now *that* could only be described in one way.

Very, very fuckable.

Without further delay, stomach flipping, heart racing, Hank hocked more spit onto his already wettened raging boner, moving so he could penetrate Mason. Gave the boy everything he had.

"Hurry up, I'm gonna cum soon, officer daddy!"

Hank needed no more words of encouragement. He placed his cock against Mason's hole, making sure it was in position before pushing it in. Mason moaned as he did so, encouraging Hank. Yet, as he thrusted, he became surprised by how easily the boy's ass relented, how it opened up for him. A moment later, his swollen knob had disappeared completely inside Mason.

When it had, Mason yelped, his voice echoing around the concrete walls of the carparking space.

Hank, not knowing what to expect, hesitated. He feared he'd hurt the boy.

"You all, right?" he had to ask.

"I'm fine! Just fuck me, officer daddy! Fuck me hard!"

Relieved, he then thrust so he went in as deeply as he could go, right to the root of his cock. Hank, already overwhelmed by all of this, had truly never felt anything like this in his life; it was like the boy's ass was sucking him in, wrapping his erection in a tight but yielding warmness that made him shudder all over. Made him ache deep inside his balls even more.

This was fucking incredible.

"Fuck!" was all Hank could manage as he began to gain his rhythm, really pounding Mason's ass, the boy's butt cheeks slapping against Hank's hips, an awesome sound along with moans, yelping, and cries of ecstasy, too, from the both of them.

What's more, while Hank fucked and fucked, with one hand he'd also grabbed the chain of the handcuffs, pulling on them, forcing Mason to arch his back so that with his other hand he could grab his long blond hair, tugging on it.

More cries of delight, more so from Mason that time. He clearly loved being dominated.

The boy then began to shudder; Hank could feel it through their connection. A moment later, Hank sweating, dripping down his brow, so close to cumming, breathless, too, the boy yelled once more, deep from his throat in what Hank could only describe as a primal scream.

Hank knew what that meant.

Mason had cum.

That realization, the sexiness of how he'd made the boy climax in such a way, made Hank release his load too. And wowsers, what a load it was, so powerful the car moved with each pulse of his release into Mason.

Hank came and came in what he could only describe as a cathartic experience, it was that mind blowing, earth shattering too.

He also yelled until he was done, his balls emptied. Hank, seeing stars for a moment, that post orgasmic blindness, realized he'd collapsed onto Mason, holding him, kissing the back of his neck.

After a moment, his breathing calming, skin cooling, Hank pulled out of his boy. Another amazing sensation, already missing the tightness he'd felt around his cock. He wanted more already.

"That was awesome," Mason said, his blue eyes dreamy within his satisfied expression.

Hank didn't reply other than to unlock the handcuffs.

As soon as they were undone, he grabbed Mason so he could hold him properly within his arms, face to face, and with plenty of tender romantic kisses.

They both kissed forever.

When that was over all too soon, Hank said, "You've jizzed all over my car."

He noticed Mason still had an erection, seemingly swooning within his loving embrace as well, Hank his world now. "I want to keep jizzing everywhere because of what you do to me," Mason said, once more his voice like before, all lust-filled and husky.

Hank was turned on too. "Then let's get up to my apartment where we can continue this."

"So much yes to that, but can I have a coffee before you fuck me again?"

"Sure—we'll both need the caffeine hit, I know it."

"We sure will."

Mason moved within their embrace so he could rub his cock against Hank's, again another lovely sensation to experience. The boy really was horny as fuck again.

As was Hank, he admitted.

When the coffee Hank brewed had been drunk, they showered together. From that moment on, they were basically attached to each other's cocks.

What a night!

Hank then fucked his boy many times, unbelieving how much he wanted it. Needed it. It was incredible.

During a break in their fucking, a time of recovery to be honest, Mason snuggling into him and running his fingers seductively through Hank's thick black chest hair, said, "Thank you for not being a chicken shit no more."

"I'm glad I'm not, my gorgeous boy."

"Ooh, I like you calling me that."

"I'm glad." Hank kissed Mason again, already missing his sensual contact, feeling himself harden even though his balls hurt because he'd blown his load that many times already tonight. "But I'm afraid our fun's over for now—I've got to get up early tomorrow. Work and all, you know."

"I understand." Mason smiled. "But can you hold me while I sleep in your arms."

"I wouldn't want it any other way."

Hank, as he felt the bliss of sleep overtake him, Mason's breathing hypnotic and lovely, hadn't felt so complete in all his life. This beautiful boy named Mason was "the one" for him.

No fucking doubt about it.

Eighth Course

The next morning well before dawn, and when showered and dressed, Hank kissed Mason tenderly on his deliciously plump lips. Lips that were not only warm and sweet, but ones that also did all those dirty things to him yesterday. Things Hank loved. The boy stirred from such attention but remained asleep in his bed. Or at least pretended to be.

Fuck, he was adorable.

"Promise I'll be back soon, gorgeous boy." Hank loved how he had a pet name for him already.

One Mason accepted too.

At that, Mason opened his eyes, those blues of his were a morning greeting Hank would never tire of. "Come back soon to fuck me hard like you did last night, my big sexy officer daddy. All right?"

"You're on." Another kiss given, one reciprocated that time.

Hank loved even more that Mason called him his daddy. A name that drove him crazy and made his cock as hard as anything in no time flat.

A dream come true.

Hank then wanted for nothing else but to rip off his clothing and hop back into bed right then, especially as Mason opened his mouth to him, giving him permission to deepen their contact. He forced himself not to do such a thing. He had business to attend to first. Namely gangsters to bring to justice seeing as he'd arranged for things to happen today at dawn.

"As much as I hate to, I've gotta go."

"I know." Mason ran his hand down Hank's arm, circling his fingers through the hairs there as he did so. "Go do your cop thing. Be a hero. Then please come back to me and be mine."

"I will, promise."

Hank left his apartment, almost reluctantly considering Mason was still warming his bed, the boy's touch lingering in his memories, wonderfully so. He realized he wanted to please his boy more than anything else, cook food for him, pamper him, do all he could to make him happy, including giving him plenty of kisses before sucking on his cock, rimming his ass, and then fucking him over and over, of course.

And aside from all the other things, the time they'd spend together from now on, the romantic shit, candlelight dinners and everything, when it came down to it sex was the glue that cemented a relationship.

Hank loved the sex he'd had with his boy and looked forward to even more.

At the same time, though, he looked forward to doing what he had to. He had other boys to rescue—boys who deserved their happy ever after as well.

As everyone deserved it.

Hank was soon parked at the designated meeting place, near enough to the warehouse to see it but not too close as to arouse any suspicion. Four other cars plus an unmarked squad van full of his colleagues, were already waiting for him.

"What took you so long?" one of the men cheekily said as soon as Hank got out of his car, sunlight only just staining the sky as it emerged above the city's skyline.

He was holding bolt cutters—part of his job was to open locked doors for this sting. That and provide support for the rest of them, naturally.

Hank decided to serve it back. "Sorry I'm a little late, Chase, but I had to thank someone for a great night last night."

"You lucky dog, you. Wish I got some..." Chase seemed to go distant for a moment, as if regretting his life choices all of a sudden. "But do tell me more—what's her name?"

Hank smiled, patting Chase on his shoulder. "His name is Mason."

Chase seemed taken aback. "I didn't know you were gay, Hank."

"I'm not, I'm bi," Hank proclaimed proudly, removing his hand off the man's shoulder. "I'm a bi guy who so happens to be in a relationship with another man right now."

Chase shrugged. "I don't get it. But hey, each to their own, right?"

"Right."

Hank then unholstered his pistol. "Are you with me, Chase?"

"I am, yeah."

"Good."

Chase then smiled. "You look happy, Hank."

"I am," he admitted, a no brainer, really.

"Say, I'd like to meet Mason when this is over and done with. We can do dinner at my place this Friday night—I'm sure he'll love my wife's pot roast as much as you do."

"You're on." Hank was glad he was with Chase, the man was a great friend as well as a good colleague. A trusted one too. "But for now, let's go bust some bad guys' asses."

Chase nodded before they proceeded to their required location at the front door of the warehouse, quick as they could while keeping low. They were a part of the leading group, Hank already organizing such a thing as he drove here.

Which wasn't much of an ask; they all knew their job, anyway.

When he was in position, however, a terrible feeling found him. A tingle at the back of his neck. Sure, this would no doubt be a surprise to the bastards, but to him everything was too quiet. He didn't like it.

Having no choice, committed really, he then signalled to Chase and the rest of them to proceed despite the growing nagging of doubt rising up within him.

Chase cut the lock with ease, the severed metal falling to the ground with a clank. When done, two others kicked down the door. Without delay, Hank ran forward, his weapon at the ready.

Inside, the warehouse was empty.

And not empty as in devoid of equipment like it was the first time that he'd seen it. No. The place was deserted.

No one here. Not even the tattooed goons of Yukkon's with all that attitude and guns at the ready.

Hank's feeling got worse.

Without further thought, stomach twisting in both fear and panic, he shouted, "Get to the cool room at the back! Now!"

The men ran on his orders, quick smart.

When at the room, Hank's heart thumped hard against the back of his ribs while he impatiently waited for Chase to cut the bolt to the cool room's door. As it was done so, *finally*, he slid it open with trembling hands.

Going inside, cautiously now because he didn't know who or what was waiting for him, letting the more armored guys go first, he heard his blood rush in his ears he was that pumped up, loving the rush.

Although what confronted Hank made him stop dead in his tracks, the rush evaporating instantly. "Get the fuck outta here!" he bellowed, while backing up and yanking Chase with him at the same time, as he'd suddenly smelt the unmistakable bitterness of almonds.

When clear of the cool room along with all the others, Chase, breathing hard and doubled over, spluttered, "Cyanide…g-gas!"

Hank's stomach dropped; the terrible feeling of before coming to the forefront. "That fucker Yukkon killed all those poor boys, the bastard."

One of the other men, hacking rasping coughs because he'd clearly taken in a breath of the gas, wheezed, "And…that's n-not…all." He gestured toward the room. "He…he's killed all of h-his…men, too."

Sure enough, Hank glancing back to the scene, witnessed the full extent of Yukkon's evil. Not only were the tattooed men dead, sprawled out on the ground, agonized looks their death mask, all the others he'd seen at that weird banquet were there as well. Dead. All of them.

Even the bald-headed man.

Hank was about to tell one of his colleagues to call the paramedics, more for them because it was too late for those in the cool room—have them checked out to make sure they were okay—when he heard the squeal of tires.

"That's Yukkon making his escape!" he cried, grabbing Chase.

Chase, seemingly all right and now running with Hank, said, "Let's get that fuckstain!"

Seconds later, the both of them were at Hank's car.

When belted in, engine started, Hank sped off with a spray of gravel from off the back tires, spinning the car around as he saw a black Mercedes up ahead in the distance. No mistaking who it belonged to.

Chase said, "I'll get on the blower to ask for the helicopter so we can track him."

"Good idea."

Driving at speed through the city and dodging the growing peak hour traffic, wasn't easy. Not one of Hank's best skills, either. Nevertheless, he did his best, surprising himself how he kept sight of the Mercedes despite red lights, trams, pedestrians, and everything else hindering him.

Yet that also surprised him.

It was almost as if the Mercedes was—

Before Hank could finish his thought, Chase observed, "If I didn't know any better, I'd say this was a decoy."

"Fuck, you're right!" Hank slammed on the brakes.

He turned the car around, heading back to the Docklands. Back to the warehouse. Up above, the helicopter could now be heard.

Chase, communicating with control, found out that the Mercedes was a decoy. The person driving it pulled over by a normal patrol car not long after Hank gave up the pursuit.

Yukkon wasn't the driver.

"Where the fuck is he?" Hank asked.

Chase relayed that to the pilot. "Sorry, lads," the pilot replied. "But I can't see any other black Mercedes within cooee of the warehouse."

Hank's spirits sank.

Chase, ever the observant one, said, "He got away."

With a huff of resignation, Hank spat. "He fucking did. What with our men affected by the gas, and Chase and me occupied by the decoy, Yukkon had plenty of time, too."

At that moment, Hank's phone rang.

It was Chief Inspector Schellenberger on the other end, no doubt about to chew Hank's ass for the complete and utter fuck up of the operation.

What was said surprised him. "I've got more bad newz for you, Inspector Riley."

Hank sighed. "And just when I thought the day couldn't get any worse."

"Indeed." The man replied. "But it seems Mister Nakamori haz also made himself scarce—his restaurant haz been burnt to zhe ground. I've got our men over zhere now, but I believe all of zhis had been planned, the fire no accident."

"Damn it!" Chase spat.

The Chief said, "I concur…but ve mustn't give up. Not until Yukkon izz found and made to pay for his crimes. I know you vill do zhis. It vill just take more time zhan you first thought."

Chase interjected, "Nothing that happens to Yukkon will come close to paying for what he's done. His crimes are too many to count."

"I know," the Chief agreed. "But ve've got to do our best, as I know you have done today. Go home, zhe both of you. Rest. Then tomorrow, ve'll tackle zhis fresh. Okay."

"Okay," Hank said. "But no lie, this has just been the shittiest day ever!"

"Amen to that," Chase agreed.

Hank couldn't help but feel for all of those poor boys. He actually began to choke up.

Chase, his voice sombre, said, "Let it all out, buddy."

He pulled over then to do what he had to while being comforted by his friend. In fact, they both cried.

Hank, frustrated and despondent, the fucked-up day taking its toll on him, truly, opened his front door, hoping beyond hope no more bad news found him today.

As soon as he did so, pocketing his keys and thinking of a cool glass of beer to wash away the bitter taste of Yukkon's evil, Mason crashed into him, holding him tightly.

"Welcome home!" the boy greeted with enthusiasm.

And with that, every single terrible thing that'd happened melted away. "You stayed here all day?"

"I did." Mason kissed Hank's cheeks and lips in turn. "I cleaned up the place a bit, and I also made dinner for us, too."

"Wow!"

The boy let Hank go. "It's going to be a while, so how about I do something special for you while we wait for it?"

Hank didn't know what to think, still feeling rather giddy and overwhelmed Mason was here, to be honest. He expected to call him later, then pick him up from his place, go on a date or something once he'd showered. He didn't expect this. Not at all.

"You've done enough..." Hank looked around his apartment. It looked great, all his muddles and messes cleaned up. "So, what else can you possibly do for me?"

Mason, his bluest blues suddenly lust-filled along with that flushed expression Hank adored, dropped down onto his knees. Before Hank could blink, the boy had fished out his cock and was sucking on it like the thing was giving him air.

And from that moment on, Hank had his happy ever after. Because there was now no fucking doubt in his mind that Mason, his innocent looking boy with the dirty mind, wonderfully so, was going to be his husband one day.

No fucking doubt.

Dessert

Some months later...

The flower shop's door opened, the sounds of the busy city beyond, tram bells ringing, cars beeping, truck engines, motorbikes, everything, flooded in from outside; the music of business. Mason had already put on his best smile for the potential customer.

The man who entered wasn't a paying one; he was wearing an Australia Post uniform complete with a fluorescent yellow high visibility vest. He held a parcel in his hand.

Mason relaxed but kept his smile. "What have you got for us today, Charlie?"

"Well, lads, looks like there's a package here for Eli today."

"For *me?*" Eli, after looking questioningly at Mason, shrugging, came around the counter stacked high with cut flowers of all types he was preparing for sale with Mason.

Mason became curious; packages sent to the shop were always addressed to him, seeing as he was the manager. Not that it mattered. But still, for Eli to receive one at work...that was different.

Charlie handed Eli a small parcel wrapped in brown paper. "Here you go, Eli. It's all yours."

Eli asked, "I wonder what it is?"

Charlie winked. "Only one way to find out, isn't there?" And with that he waved goodbye, adding, "Talk to you later, lads," before leaving the shop, the sounds of the city muffled by the closed door once more.

Eli, clearly eager, hastily opened the package. Mason went to him, now more than curious as to what it could be. But before he could get to his friend—his best mate really—to find out, Eli suddenly screamed, dropping the opened box, and staggering back until he found the counter to support him.

"What's the matter?" Mason had to ask.

Eli looked horrified, draining white, eyed wide. "Mason…it's…"

"It's what?" Mason looked down.

On the black and white tiled flooring, a trail of blood lead to a severed finger that had rolled out of the box Eli opened, a gold signet ring still on it. Mason gasped, feeling his stomach turn at such a macabre sight.

He immediately went to Eli to comfort him.

Eli shook terribly, distressed and clearly scared out of his wits. Mason couldn't blame him. He held him. Who'd even think about sending a severed finger to Eli? And more to the point, whose finger was it?

It took the longest moment for either of them to move.

When Mason managed to, hands trembling as he picked up the box and finger with tongs he'd gotten from the storeroom, then noticed that a neatly folded piece of paper had also fallen out.

"C-can...you r-read...it," Eli stuttered, still rattled.

Mason, quickly placing the finger into the box, closing the lid, heart pounding while his stomach kept turning in disgust, terribly so, then unfolded the paper. His hands still shook.

He licked his lips, plucking up the courage to continue.

What was written in neat calligraphy, almost pretty, considering the contents that came with it, was some sort of ransom note.

Mason read out loud, "Mister Eli Shigeru, I have your dear older brother Jiro in my care. If you want to see him again, you will do exactly as you are told. I will contact you soon with instructions. Don't involve the police, Hank, or your friend Mason, or the next package you'll receive will have a far more vital body part of Jiro's than a finger. Signed Yukkon."

At that moment, Eli fell to his knees and cried. "What...do they w-want from...m-me or from...Jiro, Mason? What?"

Mason, after hearing the stories his fiancé Hank had told him about the type of man Yukkon was and what sick things he did to young men, didn't want to say. All he could do for the here and now was comfort Eli.

So, comfort him, he did.

But Mason's thoughts were already turning to what he could do to help Eli and therefore his brother Jiro, despite what Yukkon wrote in the threat. Thoughts that lead him down a dark path, but one he feared he needed to walk.

To himself, he whispered so Eli—still crying, terribly

so—wouldn't hear, "I'm going to have to give Uncle Joe a call…"

The End

Author's Note

In this story I've used more traditional Japanese honorifics, especially when the gang members are referring to other people.

San = Mr/Ms and refers to adults of equal status, informally and formally.

Sama = Sir/Ma'am and refers to people of higher status (including deities, guests, customers).

Kun = Boy, bro and refers to people of junior status, boys, or amongst male friends.

Chan = Little and refers to small children, something or somebody cute, and close friends.

Tan = Refers to babies.

Senpai = Refers to a senior colleague or classmate.

Sensei = Refers to a doctor, Professor, or authority figures (teachers, lawyers, etc).

About the Author

By day I'm a humble physical therapist...and by day I'm also a writer of sweet & saucy boyslove stories (18+). I sleep at night as an old fart like me should. I'm both self-published and traditionally published. Other than that, I live with my partner and two cats and live my best life.

Website: http://konblackeboyslovewriter.com

Twitter: http://www.twitter.com/blackekon

Also by Kon Blacke
Published by Dreamsphere Books

Immortal Whispers
Kon Blacke

The Whispering Monks have foretold change to the world, and it's fast approaching. They also speak of the mortals who'll be involved.

Hereward, a lord knight who only worships the steel at his side, as the mad magician Ealdræd has taken away everyone he had ever loved. Wymond, an oblate determined to find his true self, even if it means turning away from everything he has ever known. Beornræd, a powerful magician who fears to love again after the cruelties of his past. Kieron, a stable hand with dragon blood flowing through his veins and is the rightful heir to a realm of unimaginable beauty.

All four will travel their own paths, to destroy their pasts and rebuild their future, as they thwart the evil plans of Ealdræd and his conduit, the immortal Abbot Hosho.

The whisperings continue through epic battles, both on the ground and in the sky.

The whisperings shall continue beyond the aftermath.

As it has been foretold.

More from Deep Desires Press

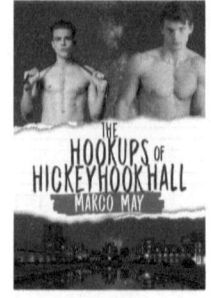

The Hookups of Hickeyhook Hall
Marco May

Jenner is gay and has a crush on Michael. Unbeknownst to him, Michael is bi and has a crush on him in return. But there's one huge obstacle in the way of professing his love. Their parents just got married to each other. Now, they're officially stepbrothers.

Both young men are determined to move on and leave their feelings behind, and what better way to do that than to dive into the challenges of starting a new life at Hickeyhook College? Their new lives are full of quirky roommates and stupid rules...and the discovery of an underground sex club with both students and staff that offers students the opportunity to cheat their way through to graduation without all the stresses of normal college life. With both young men in the club, it brings Jenner and Michael dangerously close, making it impossible to ignore the feelings they both swore to leave behind.

As sticky as their new situation is, it's about to get stickier. The powerful Dean Wicket sees the emerging relationship between Jenner and Michael and he's determined to get in the way...because he wants Michael to himself.

When the truth of Jenner and Michael comes out and the world is against them, these two men must fight with all they have to hold onto true love.